THE WORSHIPPER OF THE LEFT HAND

THE DESTINED UNIVERSE BOOK TWO

MIN HYESUNG

THE WORSHIPPER OF THE LEFT HAND

THE DESTINED UNIVERSE BOOK TWO

MIN HYESUNG

poppypub

The Worshipper of the Left Hand (The Destined Universe Book 2)
Copyright © 2021 by Min Hyesung
All rights reserved.
First published in Korea in 2021 by Gravity Books.
English translation rights arranged with Gravity Books.
Translation copyright © 2022 by POPPYPUB LLC

Translated by Alex Lee
Published by POPPYPUB, Fort Lee
www.poppypub.com
poppypub is a trademark of POPPYPUB LLC.

Library of Congress Control Number: 2022935271

ISBN (paperback) 978-1-952787-20-1
ISBN (ebook) 978-1-952787-21-8

Apostle of
Shadow

I.

23rd century AD. Humanity faced another crisis. As the land's intellectual power decreased and the population exceeded twenty billion, the planet's circulation system was broken. The rapidly increasing population and the worsening inequality between the rich and the poor put the system of society at that time in danger. The ever-changing climate and demographic threats finally demanded a solution they had been ignoring on Earth due to complacency. The solution was an exoplanet development and migration project.

Several countries launched these huge projects. Countries that could not afford to do so formed a huge consortium to support them.

Countries in East Asia and the Pacific coast generally had excellent educational traditions and technological heritage. So, China, Korea, Japan, three East Asian countries, and four Australian countries initiated their respective projects. Together, they created gigantic migration ships. About 50 to 60 percent of the ships were populated with tens of thousands of scientists, politicians, and residents of each country's nationality, while the remainder was allocated to volunteers from the countries of whichever consortium funded them. The migrant fleet project to explore and pioneer the world outside Earth, which mankind had always longed for, had come true. The migrant ships were scheduled to sail for more than 200 years at sub-lightspeed. Their destination was a group of clustered planetary systems less than 200 light-years apart. Earth's observatories had indicated that there was an 87 percent or more chance that life could survive in those settlements. It was the so-called "world of super-Earths."

Their project was a success. The *Hwanung*, which departed from Earth earlier than any other ship, settled first, followed by the *Fuxi*, the largest with 100,000 people, and the Japanese *Amaterasu*. Australia's *James Cook* arrived more than ten years later due to a route setting error. In approximately the year 2,543 AD on Earth, *Hwanung* arrived in the third planetary system. From there, they sent news of their successful migration back to Earth. If hyper-light navigation technology had not yet been developed on Mother Earth, the migrant ships would not have reached the Desirée star system for another 3,000 years.

Thus, the "Brave New World" that mankind had been longing for was created far from Earth. What was the result? Was it really paradise?

If those migrants could see the reality now, the pioneers would surely feel sad that their descendants could not change their old habits. Nearly 400 years after human settlement, madness and feuds occurred in the star system. Small within planets and large between planets. The number of small and large wars amounted to 1,000 or so in that short period of time.

We learn a lesson here. The fate of living beings is, as a philosopher on Earth said, the struggle of all against all. And it does not change no matter what world they are transferred to.

Battles and slaughter are the yokes and stigmas that are doomed upon mankind.

When we understand it, we understand how much the present system of the planetary Union is a great blessing.

It is an honor to write the foreword of this yearbook as a member of the Union. It is my hope that this book will provide an understanding of various aspects of the society and culture of the Union.

Hopefully, there will be no more Name Wars or Big Crushes.

—2915, Planetary Alliance Defense Yearbook Preface, Written by Harry Carlos

2.

Durance was a cold winter planet. It was located on the outskirts of the opposite side of the Adola system from the central quadrant of the galaxy, and at first glance it appeared so barren that no civilization would ever think of colonizing it. However, the planet was a member of the Diutin Federation. Winter and summer took turns appearing every 500 days, and cities were sparsely built in relatively moderate equatorial regions. Despite the unfavorable circumstances, the Diutin race's interest in Durance was driven by the abundance of minerals from the numerous collisions that occurred during the planet's formation, as well as the remains of ancient alien races.

It was only after Durance's weak rescue call signal broke through the enemy's jammers and arrived at Adola that a group of Diutinians went to the planet to see what had happened. Victoranus, accompanied by Dayweo and the Diutin warriors, hurried to Durance aboard several cruisers.

The warriors who reached the city through the dizzying

snow found ruined facilities. Diutin's labs and housing facilities were crumbling and falling apart.

And there were corpses or parts of corpses scattered everywhere.

Victoranus approached and examined the traces of the destruction. Blood and blizzards and corpses.

"What happened, Dayweo?" he said.

"There must have been a battle."

"There shouldn't be any more civilization in this galaxy capable of attacking our Federation. This couldn't have been the Calebs… Unless…"

"Victoranus, do you think…?"

Victoranus raised his head and looked at Dayweo. "Are you thinking what I'm thinking?"

Dayweo nodded.

"Has he come back? Proditor and his worshipers?"

"I'm not sure yet. Maybe I'm wrong. Maybe it was the pirates of the frontier?"

"Pirates messing up a planet like this? I don't know."

"I think I know. Look over there."

Dayweo pointed inside the ruined base. When Victoranus saw it, his complexion changed. The warriors who were investigating the base from the back also saw it, and froze.

Something was slowly reaching toward the sky, like a tree.

Victoranus ground his teeth. "It's the tree of life."

"We need to get rid of that, Commander."

"Yeah. Otherwise, they're going to grind us all out. Warriors, ready your swords!"

A scream pierced the air from somewhere nearby. Dayweo activated the sword from the projector on his wrist like lightning.

Dayweo saw them. The corpses were rising from the ground all over the base, like trees sprouting from the ground.

Their skin was covered in ice. Many had cuts or amputated limbs. Some had a large hole in the center of their chest. The eyes of the Diutin people, which should have given off a blue luster, were an empty dark green.

Dayweo felt as if their deaths were playing in reverse.

Corpses. Living incarnations of destruction.

Victoranus shouted, "Warriors, enter battle!"

All the Diutin warriors raised their swords. Some were controlled by a telekinetic projector on their wrist, and some were double swords with handles for both hands. The Diutin warriors moved with a speed that was invisible to the body's eyesight.

The corpses of the Diutin people roared and ran at them with a speed comparable to theirs. The earth vibrated with the sound of their footsteps.

The warriors rushed toward the corpses of their people.

Dayweo swung his sword. The sensation of the limbs of the corpses splitting apart was made him wrinkle his nose. As his left and right arms danced, the necks of the corpses flew in all directions. Hundreds of corpses approached from the right and rushed toward him. Dayweo ran right back at them and blew them away with his telekinetic power. He only wished he didn't have to hear their screams.

Swinging his sword under Victoranus, Dayweo cut off the leg of a corpse. As soon as he put the knife into the stomach of the collapsing corpse, it spun round and round. Someone threw a large thorn from his arm at him. He reflexively jumped back.

As soon as the body lost its center, Victoranus's sword

pierced its head. The skull cracked. As he ran, Victoranus blew a telekinetic wind to blow away the corpses that stood in his way.

But the bodies were endless.

The warriors cut, mutilated, stabbed, and crushed the corpses. Dayweo was soon running out of breath. It had been over an hour since the battle started. Another scream rang out. Dayweo saw one of the Diutin warriors fall, and the corpses rushed him like lightning.

As time went on, the number of warriors was gradually decreasing. There were too many corpses. The fallen warriors became corpses and rose again.

Dayweo exclaimed, "Please return them to the Mother of Civilization!"

Drenched in sweat, he stopped, looking at the horizon.

The corpses stood up endlessly, staring at him. They lined up and filled the horizon. There was an overwhelming number of them. Thousands? Maybe even tens of thousands.

"Retreat to the ship!" Victoranus exclaimed.

"Senator?"

"There are too many. We'll have to launch orbital bombardment after takeoff."

Dayweo looked at the corpses and knew that nothing else could be done.

"Warriors, retreat!" Victoranus shouted again.

The surviving warriors began to retreat toward the ships. Meanwhile, the corpses continued to rise again. Those who had lost their lives were now running with nothing but ruthless rage against living creatures. Some of the dogs were even more serious, and there were other extraordinary things that Dayweo could no longer recognize. He and the other warriors leapt tens of meters at a time with telekinetic power to escape them.

Ships flew toward them. They each boarded a cruiser. The corpses flocked to the ships, but they were all roasted in the fire from the engines. Some ships took off without any warriors on board.

Victoranus ordered the gun gates to open, as his cruiser hovered in the atmosphere over Durance.

"There may be survivors," Dayweo said at Victoranus's side.

Victoranus shook his head. "You can't find any survivors in this kind of situation. We can find them after we purify them. That's the first rule to follow when encountering a space disease, Warrior Dayweo."

Dayweo was about to say something, but then shut his mouth. He almost said to Victoranus, *So you burned all the humans ten years ago?*

Victoranus gave the order. "Each ship, warm up and prepare for bombardment."

Dayweo looked at the tree reflected on the screen. The tree of life had already penetrated the atmosphere of Durance and was heading toward space. Fear gripped Dayweo. How the hell did something like that exist in the universe?

Cosmic germs.

"Let us erase all those abominations," Victoranus said.

Jonius was the leader of the Diutin society. Overseeing more than twenty planetary systems and eighty billion Diutinians was a more complex job than that of a human head of state, and a position with incomparably enormous responsibilities. Each of Diutin's planetary systems had its own system of self-government. Among them, some were loose coalitions and some were centralized. However, at the top of all these systems was the Adola Federal Government, and the governors of each system also served as the Central Council of Diutin.

The sword of light, the peace of civilization, and the numerous small colonies and groups that were uncooperative with the central government of Adola, such as the adherents of Selim, were also broadly part of a single biological and cultural community called Diutin. The size of the world Jonius had to operate was so vast that Diutin's leader was guaranteed at least one consecutive term. This was to maintain policy coherence. Each term was six years in the Diutin calendar, and Jonius was now in his final two years of his last term of office.

In other words, it had been ten years since the former leader was ousted by the civil war. It could have felt like a short time, but after experiencing numerous events, Jonius had become a politician with a seniority unlike in the early days of his appointment.

So, he wasn't too surprised when Victoranus, once commander of the Diutin Defense Force, asked to speak to him alone.

"The Durance colony has been raided, leader," said Victoranus as soon as he sat down.

Jonius paused for a moment. "What do you mean, Victoranus?"

"A few days ago, I visited Durance with a squadron of warriors. The defense base had been destroyed, and the researchers there were either killed or disappeared. A lot of our people were harvested."

Jonius's muscles tightened. "Are you sure?"

"Certainly. We're putting the base back together, but it will take some time to stabilize the colony. The few survivors were rescued and returned to Adola. The rest were burned with the dead."

Jonius let out a groan. "That means…"

Victoran took a few deep breaths. "It looks like they're back."

"If you're sure…" said Jonius.

"I'll have to form an investigation team right now. And I'll have to issue a wartime readiness to the warriors. The same goes for the federal local troops."

Jonius stood up. "Actually, Victoranus, the sanctuary was attacked not long ago."

Victoranus was astonished. "What? Is that true, Leader?"

"Yes. The relics have been destroyed, and some crystals of the connected mind have been damaged or stolen."

Victoranus put his hand on his forehead. "Who would've done such a thing?"

"Who do you think?"

"Is that something they did too?"

"I think so," Jonius said in a determined voice. "We have to find them and clear them out."

"You're right, but before that we have to go to trial."

"Trial? You mean the council trial?"

Victoranus nodded.

"They will be watching this trial."

"Yes, the trial cannot be stopped. Isn't it already tomorrow?

Jonius made a curious expression. "What are you thinking, Victoranus?"

"We will eradicate their collaborators, Leader," Victoranus said firmly.

Jonius nodded. "Let's prepare for a counterattack. I trust you."

Aboard the *Robespierre*, the aircraft squadron was organized into two units. Squadron One was composed of many of Joshua Kwon's followers from when he was a captain in the Space Force of planet Han Ms. Mei was Joshua's lieutenant, and since the formation of the Discarded, she had served as the first flight commander.

Miyabe with red hair was called Redhead. He was an expert in electronic warfare on the *Robespierre*, and served as a counterintelligence hacker against the Allied forces.

Kyungsu was the ship's chief engineer. In addition, he was a key agency personnel responsible for the maintenance and management of the *Robespierre's* wormhole generator.

The three *Robespierre* crewmembers were gathered in the common room at the bottom of the Visitor's Tower to discuss the situation with each other. It had been a month since they wound up here in the Adola system.

Mei said, "Am I the only one who doesn't know what the captain is doing and how things are going?" She brushed her bangs. Her hair, which had not been trimmed for a month, had grown long and fell over her shoulders.

"No matter how this trial ends, I can't help but think that the *Robespierre* will be stolen by the aliens. They must be planning on taking our property," she said in a gloomy voice.

"Actually, its belongs to the aliens, right? They're sure to think they're getting their ship back," said Miyabe.

Mei sighed. "In the end, there's only one person who

might know the answer."

"Are you planning on going to Cassie?"

"Yes. I will go as our representative and ask where things are at."

So, Mei met her in Cassie's room that afternoon.

Cassie smiled at Mei and handed her some water. "Mei, what do you want to know?"

"The trial of Hypkeranos is tomorrow," said Mei. "The captain hasn't been seen for a few days. I came here out of curiosity. The crew also wants to know how things are going."

"I wish I could tell you something, but I don't even know how things are going."

"You don't know?"

Cassie nodded.

"Where is the captain?"

"In his room here in the tower. Joshua is busy studying the Diutin's book of law."

"Really? A law book?"

Cassie laughed a little. "He's in a hurry to prepare for the trial, Mei. I think he has a plan. Don't worry too much."

Joshua was startled as he scratched his chin. His beard had grown a lot and was rough. He had not left his room for several days, using all his time to study the rules of the Diutin people's trials through the alien display devices. He'd asked Dayweo to provide materials to help him prepare for the trial, and Dayweo had readily cooperated. Joshua browsed the vast amount of data he had received through the display, selected the necessary information, and recorded it in a notebook.

This trial could be a turning point that would have a big impact on the direction of the war with the Union.

He turned off the display and slowly read through his notes for hours once again, until he nodded off to sleep.

When he woke up the next morning, his ears were buzzing. He lay still and thought about what he had seen in his dream.

But nothing came to mind. Joshua felt an unknown loss. He got up and made the bed. After taking a shower, he noticed that someone had brought him clean clothes. He changed them. They must have been arranged by Diutin employees hired by the top side. He felt a small sense of wonder that the daily life of aliens was not much different from that of humans.

Joshua left the room. He boarded the transparent elevator and went down to the first floor in an instant. On the first floor, Cassie and the crew of *Robespierre* were waiting for him. Mei greeted him.

"Captain."

"Mei."

"Good luck with the trial, so that we can ride the *Robespierre* again and return to Desirée."

"Thanks. I'll do my best."

He was also greeted by Kyungsu and a hacker, Redhead Miyabe. Joshua said hello to each and every one of them.

Dayweo soon arrived. "It's time to depart, human."

"Okay." Joshua looked around. "Where is Yuna?"

"She's sleeping," said Cassie with a smile.

"Oh, right."

Joshua and Cassie boarded the alien disk-shaped vehicle, following behind Dayweo. The vehicle floated up as a shield formed around it, and started moving quickly.

It was the day of the first trial of Hypkeranos.

The disk-shaped vehicle traversed the city center of Adola. Joshua couldn't help but admire the structures of the city, which he had never seen before. The architecture was very different from the style created by mankind. Such structures were somewhat expected by Joshua, given what he'd seein in the Visitor's Tower. Nonetheless, it was astonishing to see the structures intertwined and entangled with each other according to some unknown blueprint, yet harmonized without any inconvenience. Structures with transparent textures were floating in the air, and below, citizens were roaming around on disk-type mobile devices that were moved by unknown power. Although there was no signage system, the aliens did not collide with each other as they moved in all different directions. Their complexity and speed made his eyes dizzy. Cassie was admiring it, too.

"How does traffic flow like that?" she asked Dayweo.

"Because of the connected intelligence of the machines that citizens are riding on."

"Connected intelligence?" repeated Joshua.

"I don't know how to say it in your terms. But 'connected intelligence' refers to the intelligence inherent in all machines and citizens in our society. We've developed the engineering that connects them together."

Dayweo pointed to the band he was wearing on his forehead. A crystal was shining at its center.

"This connects us to the Mother of Civilization in the Center of the Intelligence."

"What is the Mother of Civilization?"

"It is the social intelligence and the ego of our race. All

individuals are connected there, so they can know what they need at any moment. No matter what they do."

"Are you saying that all individual intellects are connected?"

"Yes. And not only the individual but also the artificial intelligences. All the intelligences of Diutin society are connected at once at all levels. Like a huge web. It's a vast network that stretches out on a cosmic scale. It evolves and expands endlessly when met. The intelligence of living things and that of artificial creatures also influence each other and evolve."

"I can't believe it. So, you're saying that—to borrow a human term—AIs and the citizens of Diutin are all connected?"

"It's similar, but a little different. But if you want me to explain it in your language in a way that's easy to understand, I have to explain it that way. It's called an artificial intelligence, but it's not a passive intelligence at all. Just like the Creator who created us, those intelligences continue to develop, and when intelligence gathers and learns from each other, it tends to fuse at some point. The same goes for transportation systems, where the intelligence of each machine and the intelligence of the user work together to calculate the optimal route for each other. That's why any sort of transportation system like you humans use—stop lights, do you call them?—is no longer needed."

"Where are those intelligences connected?" asked Joshua.

Dayweo smiled. "You have a lot of questions about us, human."

"You are our mirror. You don't know how much our race wanted to meet a different race, Dayweo. Our homeland was not originally in the three planetary systems we have today, but rather on the outskirts of the galaxy, about 30,000 light years from the center of the galaxy. We used to look at the stars and wonder how we would live if there were any other intelligent people besides us. We thought that your existence might be our future."

Cassie, who was listening to Dayweo and Joshua's conversation, said, "Weren't the Diutin people curious when they first met humanity?"

"Well, our people have never seen a civilization as advanced as ours in the galaxy. Your race's progress is quite astonishing, but that's my impression of it. Joshua, I think it's a little different from what you said. And you are not the first heterogeneous race we have encountered."

"Are there any other races in our galaxy besides humans and the Diutins?"

"Yes."

Joshua and Cassie shared a look of intrigue. "Where are they?" asked Joshua.

"You may not have seen any of them, but they are also in our society. They are living a very miserable life compared to their ancestors. But this is not a story worth telling to you. Shall we go back to the previous topic?"

Joshua looked disappointed for a moment, but reluctantly returned to the previous topic.

"What on earth can you define as a connected intelligence? Diutin society seems to depend a lot on that intelligence. Am I correct?"

Dayweo gave a troubled smile. "It's difficult to tell you exactly that right now. I don't have the time, and I don't know if it's okay to talk about this to a different race. However, our race is receiving a lot of help from society as a whole from this intelligence that we have developed over 10,000 years."

"Then why can't such a wonderful mind understand what Hypkeranos did? And, even if it was a misunderstanding, why did your kind attack our human race twenty years ago and do such a terrible thing?"

Dayweo looked straight at Joshua. "Because even the most brilliant minds cannot anticipate and comprehend everything that happens on a cosmic scale, Joshua. For the universe is chaos itself."

The speed of the disk-shaped movement mechanism slowed down. Dayweo stretched out a long hand and pointed forward.

"Here we are. I hope this time your intelligence will help Vice Captain Hypkeranos."

3.

Diutin's court of justice was in the form of a thousand discs wrapped around a round circle. In the center hall, the defendant and plaintiff's seats were placed close together. However, unlike in human courtrooms, there were no judges or jury seats. It was like an arena where the defendant and the plaintiff were watching a fighting match. Peeking up from the ground, Joshua caught a glimpse of the courthouse.

A Diutin guide came over upon seeing him and Cassie. "Hello, human. Are you here as a witness?"

Joshua nodded. "The defendant's witness."

"You can enter right now. If you open this door, you will immediately jump into the courtroom."

Light poured in as the guide opened the door. Joshua frowned slightly and then stepped through it. A flying personal vehicle suddenly appeared in front of them.

Joshua looked at the Diutin guide. "This…?"

"You can ride it."

"Okay. Cassie, take my hand."

Joshua picked up the handle sticking out of the blunt front and pulled himself onto it. Cassie, holding Joshua's hand, hopped on board behind moment.

The next moment, the colors of the lights around them changed. Joshua knew his body was under pressure. They were rising.

As the lights slowly faded away, the scenery of the courthouse he'd glimpsed from the outside unfolded around him. They had come out of the vehicle at some point. Cassie patted him on the shoulder and pointed to one side. In front of them were two chairs. They sat down, and some Diutinians glanced at them.

A voice carried to their ears.

"…Therefore, it can be said that the components of these acts are extremely narrow-minded and subject to misuse, and considering the organic flow of the case, I think that the guilt of the accused must be taken seriously."

"Wait. Human witnesses have arrived."

A Diutin in the center of the courtroom, with wavy hair and a band around his head studded with blue crystals, raised his hand. He looked like a judge. He pointed to Joshua and Cassie. The person who had just been speaking stopped talking. Joshua thought he must be the prosecutor.

Joshua took his eyes off them, looked to the other side, and found Hypkeranos sitting calmly. Hyp glanced at Joshua and Cassie and nodded. Joshua nodded back.

The Diutin who appeared to be a judge took a seat in the stand and spoke to Joshua. "I am Dunas. I am the moderator of this trial. This here is Councilor Giltarion, and he has been tasked with the prosecution of the accused. Everyone's heard about you, but this is the first time a human has ever come to court here. Could you introduce yourself briefly?"

Joshua got up and straightened himself. He cleared his throat once and opened his mouth. "I wonder if you can understand my language."

"Don't worry about the language. We have an interpreter speaker installed so that your language is translated as soon as you speak. Don't you understand our language too? Same principle."

"Okay, Commander. So, let's get started. I'm Joshua Kwon, the captain of the *Robespierre*, and the leader of the Discarded Resistance in the Desirée system. The woman who came with me is Cassie Ice, my partner. We are witnesses on the side of the accused, Hypkernaos."

He paused for a moment, then spoke again.

"And the defender of Hypkeranos."

Some Diutinians murmured behind him. Joshua looked at Hyp and noticed that he was a little withdrawn.

"I don't know if it's a coincidence," said Dunas with a smile, "but this first trial is a council trial. Unlike a normal trial, a council trial does not have much to do with formality. So, I can ask a question, and the prosecutor over there may ask a question. Or, the members of the council who are attending the trial over here can ask and answer any number of questions. There is not one prosecutor. On behalf of the government, members of the council's ruling Truth Alliance have formed a prosecution team. A witness can defend the defendant or attack him. He can speak in any way, as long as it's not too extreme, aggressive, or time-consuming. Do you understand?"

"I understand. It's a little different from the way trials in our world work, but I think it'll be more fun. As long as I'm not off topic, I can testify, defend, or conversely, ask questions to the prosecutors, right?"

"You understood the court rules well." The moderator suddenly erased the smile from his face and spoke in a low voice. "Then, let's get started. Are you in agreement?"

"Fine."

"Okay, let's start with the prosecution team first. Who has a question?"

Lights came from the lower part of the discs surrounding the courthouse. A red crest of two crossed swords stood out.

"Please state your position and name," Dunas called to the councilmember with the light on.

"I'm Diane, a member of the Truth Alliance."

"Okay. Let's get started."

Councilor Giltarion half-turned toward Diane, to show he was listening. Hyp also looked at Diane.

Diane opened her mouth. "Hypkeranos, you are a warrior who made an oath to the Mother of Civilization. Wormhole technology is one of the core technologies of our civilization, and giving it to a different race is an act of betraying our race. Were you aware of this?"

"Dear Senator Diane, I have never betrayed the Mother of Civilization. It was not an act that benefited a different race or endangered our people. It is out of sheer compassion and pity for the poor people who have been subjected to unjust violence."

"You're talking about motives. But I'm talking about consequences, and the nature of this trial is also a place to discuss the consequences of what you've caused. For the first time, humans are sitting in our courts. Aren't they trying to overthrow their government with tech ships?

This is our involvement in their history. And there is no guarantee that one day they will not become a threat to our civilization."

"Senator, to be clear, the race called humans also developed wormhole navigation technology. They did so much later than us, but it was developed by their own abilities anyway. It is true that I gave them our ships and technology, but in the light of their capabilities, it was by no means a change in the course of history. They haven't been able to build a ship equipped with wormhole navigation technology in over ten years, but it's only a matter of time. And threats are always the standard by which the hostile side is judged first. I don't think there will be any war or discord if we offer them goodwill."

Cassie whispered to Joshua, "Ten years ago?" Her brow was furrowed in confusion.

Joshua glanced at her. "Because one year in the Adola system is like two years in our world." Cassie nodded in understanding.

Hyp's powerful voice filled the courtroom.

"Providing ships and technology is merely a material reward. If humankind was a civilization that did not attain such technology on their own, then I think you would be right. Isn't it better to see it as war reparations?"

Giltarion clicked his tongue. "War reparations are officially between governments, warrior. If you are right, you should have compensated their government. Why did you offer compensation to this man and his people, specifically? They use our ships to fight their government. It is a violation of the Civilization Charter, which states that we must not interfere in the internal affairs of a heterogeneous race. Do you deny it?"

Hypkeranos didn't say anything. Joshua knew that Hyp had been weighed down by Giltarion. Joshua looked at Cassie, and she nodded.

He cleared his throat. "Moderator Dunas, I want to speak."

The moderator looked at Joshua in surprise, as did Giltarion.

"Chief Director," said Giltarion, "are you going to allow the remarks of different races?"

Dunas smiled mischievously. "There's nothing wrong with that, Senator. Let's hear it."

Giltarion shook his head. The moderator didn't seem to notice it.

"Tell me, human. Please state your position first."

Joshua pondered for a moment what the moderator meant, then understood. "This is the position of the accused."

"Good."

Joshua coughed. "I am from a planet called Han. Ten years ago, twenty years ago in our system, your ships attacked my planet. Diutin's mighty battleship slaughtered a third of my hometown's population. The essence of this trial is not about leaky technology. This trial is wrong. The subject of the trial should be about your war crimes. Because we are here. And you deserve to be held accountable for that sin."

Giltarion shouted, "Ignorance!"

Joshua spotted Aureus frowning at the back of Giltarion. He also saw an alien taller than the nearby lawmakers a little farther away with his chin raised and an interesting expression on his face. That was better than anger, at least.

Diane said in a voice colder than metal, "Stop speaking,

man. This is Diutin's court. You are a witness, not a prosecutor."

"Senator, do you agree that I can accuse you and your government?"

"I don't agree."

"Why not?"

"Because it was an accident."

"Oh, an accident? What does the word 'accident' mean here? Is it an accident in the sense that it was unintentional, or does it mean that it was an event that means nothing to you, whether many people died or not?"

"Human!" Diane shouted, and the other councilmembers murmured to each other.

Joshua glanced at Hyp. His expression was darker than anything he had ever seen. From Joshua's point of view, it was clear that Diane was holding back her anger. *You'll have to.* Joshua snorted. *How would you feel if you were attacked by a lower race the way we were?*

"Human, the attack happened because you declared war first. Also, our administration was in a very chaotic situation. It was an unusual situation in which barbarism that our kind would not normally show was unleashed. The government had a problem with legitimacy. Our current government is completely different. You have to understand that."

"My name is Joshua, not 'human,' Senator. I don't care how the character of your government has changed. I'm just talking about the adverse effect your actions have had on us. As you just said, I am here right now. I'm talking about the actions of the Diutin fleet and their consequences."

Diane flinched. The murmur of the councilmembers

grew louder. Voices called out:

"This is nonsense!"

"That man is insulting the Mother of Civilization!"

The moderator raised his voice. "I ask the members of the council to be quiet."

Then he looked at Joshua. "Although our trial format is relatively free, this is a courtroom and not a meeting place, Joshua Kwon. Please state your intentions more clearly."

"Okay, sir. What I want to say is this."

Joshua looked around the courthouse once from left to right and from right to left. As he brought out the words that had been hidden inside him for twenty years, he felt an unknown core bursting out.

"I lost my wife, children, and colleagues. They never saw another tomorrow because of the slaughter that happened on that day—the slaughter you call a neglectful 'accident.' You who sit here are members of the galactic planets of the great Diutin race. Me and my partner here stand alone on behalf of our planet. Hypkeranos is the only alien who acknowledged the suffering we experienced and apologized to us, at least as far as I know. He was the only Diutin with a conscience. You are not entitled to discuss his guilt. Not a day goes by when I and all the other survivors of the attack on Han don't go to sleep wishing we could see the faces of those we lost just on more time." His voice shook with grief and fury. "I demand that from this first council trial to the rest of the trial, the prosecution adds a charge of extraterrestrial genocide for the Diutin Federation."

4.

The next day, Danny neatly dressed in his uniform and went to Harry's house.

Harry was also dressed in a well-ironed uniform. The attendant prepared tea and refreshments. It was past three o'clock, an hour after Danny got there, when the attendant announced that a guest had arrived. A private aircraft lowered into the yard of the residence. The four A-wings of the security unit landed together behind the white aircraft. Danny watched them through the gap in the drawing room curtain.

He recognized that the white aircraft belonged to the President. It was a smooth metal that no plasma or even the most powerful electromagnetic rail gun could penetrate. Danny quickly pulled the curtain in case anyone outside noticed him peeking.

Ten minutes later, the door opened and two men entered. One was silver-haired, tall, and wearing casual clothes and a coat. Danny thought the President looked more assertive in person than he did on a display screen or when seen from a distance. The man next to him wore glasses and a khaki overcoat. He had to be the President's chief of staff, Sura Handler.

Harry and Danny salute at almost the same time.

"Sir. It is an honor to have you here," said Harry.

The silver-haired man walked up to Harry and tapped him on the shoulder. "Don't be formal, Harry. I'm here to talk to you in person." He looked at Danny, who stood behind Harry. "This is your grandson. Nice to meet you, Captain. I am Amon Soros."

Danny had seen the President from afar at a mobile flyer screening commemorating the tenth anniversary of the annexation of Valhalla a year ago. At that time, the President had made a solid and thorough impression. Danny felt like he was back in time, seeing the President's short swept hair and protruding cheekbones. Between them, deep but penetrating eyes stared at Danny. Even now, the President had unchanging passion and will.

This was the most powerful man in the Desirée system. The Iron President, Amon Soros.

"It is an honor, sir," said Danny.

"You're a handsome young man. You belong to the Hound Dog Squadron?"

"That's right."

"It's a proud name. Isn't it a symbol of honor? Not to mention, you're the Connecticut hero. It must have been a difficult task to subdue Joe. I was actually thinking of deploying a riot squad at the time. Anyway, I'm glad there are talented people like you. "

"Thank you, sir."

"But how was such a talented man caught by the enemy

this time?"

Harry put on a puzzled expression. Danny glanced into the President's eyes, but the President didn't have a hard expression on his face. Danny counted to three before answering.

"I didn't pay attention."

"It could be because they have an overwhelming number of capable people. It is clear that the Resistance has better telekinetic skills than us, and many more of them who possess such powers, as well."

The President sat on the sofa. The chief of staff, who had been quietly listening from the side, sat in the chair next to him. The President motioned for Harry and Danny to sit down as well, and they did so.

"You talked a lot with Jinsoo Kim, Captain?" asked the chief of staff.

"Yes, sir. In fact, it was a conversation, not just an interrogation."

"Was it just a normal conversation?"

"No. He tried to recruit me, talking about my uncle Yeonsu Carlos and Karl Ryoma, the Third Regiment Commander."

Sura Handler laughed. "You are so honest, Captain Carlos."

"I'm just telling the truth."

The President intervened. "Captain, what exactly did he say to you? Give me a summary of all the things he said."

Danny's pulse was beating fast. He looked at his granfather, and Harry nodded. The President was waiting for Danny's story.

"Then I will filter out unnecessary things as much as possible and tell you only the core," said Danny.

He started talking. He told them the story of the origin of mankind, and the escape of Yeonsu Carlos and Karl Ryoma, and Jinsoo's requirements for the independence of each planet. Danny had no choice but to look at the President's eyes, hoping he wouldn't notice the bead of sweat trickling down the back of Danny's neck. However, the expression on the president's face was surprisingly peaceful. It was so relaxed that Danny doubted whether he was even listening to him.

But he didn't say anything about the Big Crush.

After the conversation was over, the chief of staff said, "He was trying to convince you, Captain."

"It seems so."

"Why did he let you go so easily?" The chief of staff wore a cold, irritable expression on his face. His eyes were as gray as an oil-soaked engineer's handkerchief. "You must have thought of that, right?"

Harry coughed and intervened, standing. "Sir, my grandson is, to be honest, a bit of an idiot. He doesn't think clearly at the best of times."

Danny snorted inwardly. *That's the warmest evaluation you can give of your grandson?*

The President also smiled, as if he felt the same way. "Harry, your grandson is also a captain of the Allied forces. Your evaluation is too low. I understand it with humility. What the chief of staff wanted to talk about was what Jinsoo Kim was thinking when he released Captain Carlos."

"They seemed to think I would end up on their side in the end," Danny said, standing as well, and the other three men turned to him.

"Why do you think he said that, Captain Carlos?" said

the chief of staff.

"I think it was because of my uncle, Lieutenant Colonel Carlos. And…"

"And?"

Harry gave Danny a sharp look, as if to say, *Don't.*

Danny ignored him. "He said the Union government caused the Big Crush."

Harry let out a strange moan.

The President took a few sips from the mug in front of him. "The Union government caused the Big Crush? That's funny." He put down the teacup. "Let's all sit down, especially Harry. This atmosphere is chaotic. Let's talk comfortably. Captain Carlos, you too."

Harry looked at Danny, but Danny turned away. Harry sat down in his own personal chair, and Danny sat down too.

Sura Handler was looking at Danny with intense eyes. "Anyone with eyes and ears can see the audiovisual data recorded in the Union Archives in real time. The aliens and their ships that attacked planet Han at that time were not Allied camouflage."

"Jinsoo Kim seemed to believe it was the Union government that led the aliens to attack planet Han."

"You're kidding!" The President let out a short laugh. "Can you imagine?"

Danny sighed. He wasn't getting anywhere with them.

"Let's assume that's the case, Captain. We'll go over the methodical details of how the Diutinians attacked planet Han, but let's assume that's really the case for now. What will that mean for the Union?"

"Your Excellency will be in trouble. It is an act of betrayal against Desirée humanity."

"Be careful, Danny Carlos," Harry rebuked Danny in a strong tone.

The President waved his hand. "No, Harry. Danny is right. May I call you Danny, Captain?" Danny nodded. "Thank you. Danny, you are just telling the truth. Keep talking. What else will happen if this betrayal is true?"

"The civil war will intensify, sir. The Discarded, the Roots, the pirates of Valhalla, the Ganesh government. These are the forces that are already hostile to the Union and form the Resistance. There, planet Han can rise even in the third planetary system."

"It will be eleven years since the Planetary Union government unified the Desirée system in its perfect form, and we will be standing in the middle of turbulence. Is that what you mean, Danny?"

"That's right."

"Then what should I do?"

"If it's true, we must make sure that information is never leaked. And if it's false, it's simple. We must wipe out the insurgents for good. Either way, speed is life, sir. The voices of doubts about the Union government will grow wildly in the air. Those voices might be lifeless at first, but at some point, they will gain vitality beyond their control. Take all the fleets in New Shanghai right now. We must attack Ganesh."

The President smiled as if he liked it and said, "Jinsoo Kim didn't know who you really are."

Harry look at his grandson with some surprise. He felt both admiration and nervousness at the sight of his grandson.

"Is a planetary uprising likely to happen?" asked the President.

"Maybe yes, maybe no. Whether or not the public is aware of these facts is important. Therefore, it is important to minimize and monitor external inflows to all the Union planets. Especially Han."

"Well, I think Chief Handler has something to say about that."

The Chief of Staff sipped on the tea the attendant brought him and said "The Han autonomous government is fully cooperating with us. Even with these commotions going on right now. That's nothing to worry about, Captain."

Sura Handler's gray eyes darkened even more.

"Captain, do you know Yuri Ivanova?"

Danny hesitated. "I have to answer the truth, sir? I'm guessing more investigations have already been conducted than I thought."

The chief of staff looked at Danny without a word.

"That's right. I met her in a place I frequented. Yuri Ivanova was the owner, and she was with the Discarded. I didn't realize until the Discarded raided Altra. It felt like a blow to the head."

"So, do you know that she is now commanding the Discarded on behalf of Joshua Kwon, and is also the captain of the flagship *Moscow*?"

Danny blinked at him in surprise. "No, sir. Is that true?"

Sura Handler chuckled. "I guess you didn't know, Danny. It's true. She's now the commander-in-chief of the Discarded. I don't know where Joshua Kwon went. The *Robespierre* hasn't been found either. That woman and Jinsoo Kim are in charge now."

"She's bigger than I thought." Danny let out a short laugh.

"Is that funny?" At the President's words, Danny realized he was smiling.

"It's not that kind of laughter, sir. It's more like a laugh out loud because the situation is so unbelievable."

"Were you close?"

Danny didn't know what to say to that. He'd had a major crush on Yuri.

Danny loved Yuri Ivanova.

"Yes, sir."

He remembered that night. His figure was reflected in the fresh mint sparkles of the evening dress. Would she think of him now? Had she really wanted to dance with him that day, or was it all just a ploy to get close to him?

Maybe both.

A crow tattoo on the inside of her leg came to mind. The crow's eyes seemed to come to life, as if laughing at a stupid man.

"…do it, Danny."

He'd missed the first part of what the President said.

"What?"

The President looked at him expressionlessly. "I told you to capture Yuri Ivanova."

Danny's stomach twisted into knots.

"I've heard they're going to Neptunus, Captain," said the chief of staff. "You must get ahead of them."

"Neptunus?" Danny repeated. "Are you talking about Neptunus? It sounds like you're talking about New Sydney's moon, sir."

"Yes. Yuri Ivanova will go to Neptunus."

"What is there? Why are they going to Neptunus at such an important time?"

"There is a secret research facility that very few know

about," said the President. "A place where biological weapons are made and tested. Commander, you should know. Lists of weapons with only codes starting with the unique number E."

Harry's body trembled. Danny saw his grandfather's eyes widening.

"Sir, is it alien technology?" asked Danny, his heartbeat picking up.

"That's right."

"On Neptunus…"

"Indeed. Isn't it the best place to experiment? A place with nothing but water and huge protozoan sea creatures. A planet with controlled access."

Danny asked cautiously, "What sort of technology is it exactly, sir?"

The President gave a knowing smile. "It's a biological technology that can finally change the course of this war. A technology brought by aliens who appeared from deep space and visited New Shanghai. Captain, you've heard of those stories, right?"

"Yes, but I thought they were made up."

"It's not fiction. The previous Union administrations have interacted with aliens."

"Were they Diutinians?"

"No more, Captain."

The chief of staff intervened. "You and the members of the Third Regiment, including those of the *Little Boy*, will follow my command from now on. Of course, my command is, in effect, the will of the President. Go and capture Yuri Ivanova. Bring her back to us alive."

Danny straightened his stance, nodding. "I will."

Harry had a look on his face like something was wrong.

"Chief Handler, thank you for giving my grandson an important task, but how do you know where the Resistance is going? Besides, they have good ships. I think you should give them more support."

"We will, Commander."

"What do you mean?"

"If you meet Yeoreum Granot, she will help you."

Danny looked at him "Isn't that the president of the Granot Group?"

"Yes. The company that made the handy tools, weapons, and spaceships you use. She's going to give you a ship that can navigate wormholes."

Seeing Danny's surprised expression, the President smiled. "Why are you surprised? It's just a remake of what the Mining Union already made twenty years ago," he said cheerfully. "Good luck, young friend. Your uncle has already taken one of our precious ships, so you have to use it and return it. Okay? They're going to be mass produced."

With that, President Soros and his chief of staff left with their bodyguards, faster than when they had arrived.

Danny watched through the drawing room window as the private plane and the A-wings took off. Then he turned to Harry.

"Do you know? What are the alien technologies?"

"Didn't you just hear that it's a secret, Danny?"

"Yes, I did hear that. I'm not as stupid as you think. I was just asking. You've kept a lot of secrets from me already." Danny crossed his arms and gave his grandfather a pointed look.

Harry sighed. He was quiet for a long time, and then he spoke again. "It is not recorded exactly when the aliens appeared. It is usually said at least 150 years ago, when the Union was made up of only New Shanghai and New Sydney. People say they may have been the same alien group as the Diutinians. But no one knows for certain. Anyway, the aliens came bearing a container with a mysterious energy source. It was sealed really tight. It's still unknown what exactly the energy is. I've heard that they haven't been able to figure it all out. But I saw it once. It's denser than any other energy source known to human-kind, and it is far stronger than any other kind of energy. Technology forbidden by God. The power to destroy lives."

Danny's brow furrowed. "I beg your pardon?"

"The alien technology—that energy source—can blow up a planetary system. I'm sure of it. I saw it firsthand on the planet Han that fateful day. Their technology has even changed the natural environment of the planet, which used to be far richer."

Danny's mind was racing to understand this. "And the Union has this energy source? Where are they keeping it?"

"It must be on Neptunus. I don't know what else they might be keeping there; I don't know the details of what research was conducted after Sura Handler overhauled the research facility. That's all I know. Danny, I don't fully understand what the President is planning, but your mission is an important one. Make sure to capture Yuri Ivanova."

Danny didn't say anything.

"It's going to be all right," said Harry, standing and grasping his grandson's shoulder. "You've got the latest ship, and you'll get help from Yeoreum Granot. You'll like her, too."

"Why do you say that?"

"They said she was a beauty."

5.

When Desmond was escorted to the fourth-floor end room of Hotel Three at Ganesh Spaceport, he found more people there than he expected. Karan, who was busy talking to his subordinates, patted the seat to him.

"Sit down, Desmond. Don't panic."

"There are more people here than I thought, Captain. Do you want to play cards?"

Theresia growled at him. "New Sydney jokes are no fun, Desmond."

"Why would I be joking? Jokes are reserved for those with a good heart, so you don't deserve to hear one."

"Why, you—"

Jena interrupted their conversation. "Stop it, Theresia. Desmond, you too. We're not here to joke."

Desmond sat down on the empty single-seater chair. Karan handed him a beer, and he took it and swallowed it.

"Is the ship maintenance work going well?" asked Karan.

"No problems so far. Customization is complete, and

once the weapons are loaded, Admiral Lionel's battleship will be freely available as your flagship. The agency and crewmembers are also in the final stages of restructuring. It seems that it will take some time to reset the crew of *Canberra.*

"Good job. Now, tell us what's on Neptunus."

Desmond flinched. "Neptunus?"

"Yeah. That sea planet."

"Why are you curious about Neptunus, Captain? What does Neptunus have to do with this war?"

"Are you answering my question with a question? To put it simply, it seems like a separate platoon will be formed and sent to Neptunus. They say there is a secret research facility there run by the Union. They say the facility's holding something that can change the course of war. Have you heard anything about that, Desmond? You're from New Sydney, and you were an Allied officer. You think you know something?"

Desmond looked desperate, like he was cornered.

Theresia whistled. "Seeing how timid he looks, he knows something for sure. Desmond, what is it? Is there anything else besides giant sea creatures on Neptunus?"

Karan smiled at him. Sweat trickled down the back of Desmond's neck.

"Tell us what you know, Desmond," said Judy.

All the pirates were staring at Desmond. He sighed, and began to speak with a look of disapproval. "There are secret research projects in the Union that start with the codename E."

"Codename E?"

Desmond nodded. "Yes. Codename E. I don't know what the letter E stands for. I don't know, and I don't want to know. All the Allied soldiers who served in Valhalla and New Sydney know something about it. I heard some strange rumors. It's absolutely imperative that you avoid dispatching to Neptunus."

"Why?" asked Theresia. "Do people complain about the workload there?"

Desmond didn't smile as he looked at him. " Once you're sent there, it's hard to come back. No one knows why. But most of those sent there choose it as their place of work, and they don't transfer anywhere else. It's like a permanent move."

Gain tilted his head with a curious look. "Then, isn't that a good thing? You're saying that the working environment is that good?"

"People who go there never come back. People who change their job to Neptunus don't go to another job after that."

"Wait, what are you saying, Desmond?" said Jena, frowning. "It's just a change of work, isn't it? Can't you go and visit these people, or contact them by some other means, so you'll know what's going on with them?"

Desmond looked at Jena with gloomy eyes. "Contact? You would think so, yeah. Some of my colleagues went to Neptunus, and I tried contacting them but never heard back. I contacted their families, too. I even went directly to my superior to ask for permission to go there, but I didn't get it. Neither soldiers nor civilians are allowed to visit Neptunus. And the people who transferred there, I never heard from them directly again. Their families said the same thing. They're not coming home."

Karan held up a hand to intervene. "Wait, Desmond. If what you're saying is true, it's unclear if these people are even alive. Is that what you're getting at?"

"No, they must have been alive, because we could see them during our regular interstellar training sessions."

"Training? So, the ones who were dispatched to Neptunus showed up during training?"

"Yes. As if nothing had happened." Desmond bit his lip. "But they were no longer the colleagues we knew."

"I don't understand. What do you mean?" Theresia had a serious expression on his face.

"The soldiers sent to Neptunus didn't recognize us any more. When we asked if they were doing well, the expressions on their faces were incomprehensible. They acted like they were seeing us for the first time. They didn't know us any more. But I don't think it was an act. It was as if all their memories had been lost. It was obvious that the Union government had done something to them. It wasn't just us who thought so, but also their relatives. Of course, husbands and wives were there. The training was secret but some of my colleagues who noticed how the Neptunus soldiers were different leaked information. And the Neptunus soldiers didn't even recognize their own family."

A chill slid down Gajin's spine, though the temperature control in the room was working.

Desmond continued, "The soldiers who conducted the joint defense and maneuver drills went back to Neptunus after the training was over. We don't know what happened to them. One of my pals, he tried to go with them. He snuck onto the ship. It was treason, in a way, but he did it because his friend had gone to Neptunus and he had to know what was going on."

"What happened to him?" asked Gajin.

"He didn't come back. We thought he was dead. It

seemed like the only possible outcome. Then one day, he showed up."

Jena was watching Desmond intently. "Did he not remember anything?"

"He looked like an idiot. He was having a lot of trouble in his daily life, because he couldn't even remember his own name. He became morbidly afraid of the dark. He always had nightmares, where there was even the slightest shadow. He didn't want to go anywhere at nighttime. In fact, he became an asshole."

Desmond had a gloomy look on his face as he recalled his old friend.

"I'm not quite sure what's on Neptunus, but I have a guess. He must have witnessed the codename E project. I'd love to know what happened there, but now I'll never get him to tell me."

"Why not?"

Desmond pretended to point a gun at his head.

"Because my friend blew his head."

When Junkou opened his eyes, he saw the Haneul looming above him.

"Junkou?"

"Haneul? Where am I?"

Haneul Bravo took Junkou's face in her hands, kissed him on the forehead, and looked around.

"Oh! It hurts. What are you doing?"

"Okay. Just hold on, you idiot." Haneul's voice was trembling. Junkou stopped struggling.

"Is this some kind of hospital? Is my body healthy? It's not like I'm falling apart or crippled?"

"Shut up, you idiot. You'll be fine."

Junkou closed his eyes and embraced the Haneul with both arms. When he opened them, he noticed a tear trickling down Haneul's cheek.

"Is Dallas dead?"

Sky nodded. Junkou was quiet for a long moment.

"We tried to save as many pilots as possible," said Haneul. "But you couldn't save Dallas, Meg."

"I thought so. I saw the captain's fighter crash. We couldn't stop the Allied fleet."

"I'm glad you survived, Meg. Nearly half of the squadron members were killed. I don't know how, but the radio waves from that transport made the fighters go of control. You only survived because the trees caught you."

"I'm so exhausted, Bravo."

"I know, Junkou."

"Just a few hours ago, I was counting how many Dallas and planes we shot down. But now he's dead and I'm barely alive."

Haneul hugged him tightly. "Don't say anything, Junkou. Don't say anything."

She kissed Junkou. Junkou could taste her tears. Haneul lifted him gently onto the bed and then turned away.

"Where are you going?"

"To report the damage. Rest until I come back. It'll take a few hours."

Junkou closed his eyes as he watched the slender waist of the Haneul disappear.

Yukyung heard a voice in the dark. It was a man's voice. Yeonwoo's voice. He was shouting for her to go. "Get out!" he screamed. "Run away from this darkness!"

All around her was water.

And pain.

"Yeonwoo!" Yukyung cried.

She tried to move in the direction she'd heard his voice. She swam through the water into the deep sea. In the water, the creatures looked like they had gone blind. They were floating and moving their tentacles to and fro as Yukyung passed. A few of them followed her.

Pain.

Yeonwoo's voice resounded in the fishy water. Yukyung discovered an underwater cave.

"Don't come this way!"

Yukyung saw piles of rotten seaweed. The cave grew deeper and deeper, and more and more seaweed appeared.

Something was swaying to and fro in one of the rotten piles. Shaking like a relic in a forgotten time, it looked like a corpse of a living creature scattered in the water. Yukyung frowned.

All kinds of living things were sticking their snouts around the shaking object.

Creatures were devouring it.

The object changed into the shape of Yeonwoo. Yeonwoo, with his organs exposed, was being devoured. His head, which had been looking down at his bones and organs being eaten, moved and looked at Yukyung, his mouth gaping. Yeonwoo raised his hand and stretched it out to Yukyung. The hand had only a few fingers left.

So much pain.

The snouts that were devouring Yeonwoo followed his hand and looked at Yukyung.

The snouts had no eyes.

Yukyung woke up with a shriek, by bouncing her body as if jumping out of the water.

Her lungs were filled with excruciating pain. It felt as if the joints and bones in every corner of the body were being beaten with a club. The light was so intense that she couldn't open her eyes. Yukyung reflexively covered them with both hands and lowered her head. All sorts of unbearable stimuli were trying to invade her senses. It was too much.

"Ahhh…!" she screamed.

She was going to die like this.

A sound reached her ears amidst all the flooding sensations.

"Yukyung! Are you okay?"

Involuntarily, she opened her eyelids slightly. Blurred images slowly took shape. Tears spurted out.

It took some time and pain for her eyes to fully perceive the environment around them. But she soon realized she was in a hospital room.

The woman looking at her was someone she knew.

"…Ari?"

"You've come to your senses!"

Yukyung tried to sit up, but she couldn't. After noticing her intentions, Ari grabbed her hand and helped her get up.

"Is this a hospital?" Yukyung's voice cracked.

"Yeah, Ganesh National Central Hospital. You've been lying in this bed for quite some time."

"For how long?"

"It's been a month."

"One month?"

She couldn't believe that. How could she have been lying in bed for so long?

"Wait a minute! Let me call some people."

Ari hurriedly left the hospital room. Yukyung sat in dismay, enduring the prickly pain, trying to understand reality.

The first person who came in was Jinsoo. He appeared with the doctors and nurses, looked at Yukyung's face, and then hugged her. It was embarrassing and suffocating.

Jinsoo pulled away and looked into her face. "Are you awake? Do you remember your name?"

"Yeah."

"I'm glad. You should have slept a little more. How do you feel?"

She shrugged. "I'm alive."

"Do you remember what happened last?"

"I escaped from Neptunus. My fiancé, Yeonwoo, is dead. I brought Hogan here."

A bitter taste filled Yukyung's mouth. She swallowed it down, then said, "Where's Hogan? You haven't left him alone, have you?"

"He's in quarantine, Yukyung," said Ari, who appeared behind Jinsoo. "He can't get out."

"Are you sure? Where is the containment facility?"

"You don't have to worry about that," said Jinsoo. "It's a facility provided by the Ganesh government. A lot of things have happened while you've been asleep. The Resistance has progressed quite a bit. I think it's better if you rest a bit more first. We'll talk about it later."

Jinsoo got up from her bed. He said a few words to the doctors and nurses who had come with him, and they nodded. Just as Yukyung was about to panic, the doctor said that glucose and sleeping pills would enter her body. They said she would wake up refreshed in a few hours.

Yukyung couldn't lift her body. She surrendered herself

to the darkness once again.

A few hours later, Yukyung opened her eyes to see Jinsoo and Ari in her room again. Next to them were a woman and a man she didn't recognize.

The woman introduced herself. "Hello, Yukyung. I'm Yuri Ivanova from the Discarded. How are you feeling?"

"I'm okay. Just very weak."

Yuri nodded and pointed to the man next to her. "This is Karan Shetty of the Red Wind Brotherhood. I'm sure you've heard the name."

Yukyung was ashamed of herself for opening her mouth like a fool for a moment. She turned her head toward Jinsoo. "Are the pirates helping us?"

"Could you call me Brotherhood, Miss?" Karan said with a smile.

Jinsoo reluctantly nodded. "These are the people who have been very diligent in helping us, Yukyung. They are on our side."

"Yes. And I'll be part of the expedition," said Karan.

"Expidition? To where?" asked Yukyung.

Jinsoo and Yuri looked each other.

"Yukyung, we're going back to Neptunus," said Jinsoo.

"You want to go there again?" said Yukyung weakly.

"Yes. So, you have to tell me. What did you see there?"

As Karan spoke, Yukyung looked at him with unfocused eyes.

Yuri was watching her carefully. "I'm sure it's hard to revisit the past, but do you remember what happened there? Anything you can remember will help."

Yukyung looked at Yuri, but instead of Yuri, she saw Yeonwoo. No, to be precise, she saw a large snout that chewed and swallowed Yeonwoo. She saw the twisted creatures that threw their bodies on top of him. Her man was dead. Did digestion end in the monster's stomach? He had been swallowed whole, so his limbs would still be attached.

She was fading fast. In her dreams, she saw eyeless creatures devouring Yeonwoo.

The world had gone far away. As her sense of reality disappeared, the sights she had seen became realistic and appeared and disappeared before her eyes. Yukyung knew she was screaming.

It was a sharp scream that seemed to tear her lungs.

6.

It was the day of the second trial. Someone spoke to Joshua as he was walking down the yard in front of the courthouse, with Cassie a few steps ahead of him.

"Hello, Joshua Kwon."

The person speaking to him was a Diutinian wearing a bright emerald robe. He was tall for a Diutinian.

"Hello. Who are you?"

"I am Gartrail, Councilor of Nanat."

Joshua remembered him. He was the Diutinian who'd sat quietly in the courtroom during the first trial, with an interesting expression on his face.

Gartrail held out a hand. "Nice to meet you. Are my words being translated properly?"

"Yes, they are." Joshua took his hand.

After he lowered it, Gartrail said, "I wanted to talk to you before the trial, human. Adola is very noisy right now because of this trial. Since you are in the Visitor's Tower, you may not be aware, but it has caused quite a bit of commotion and uproar in Adolan society. I think it's been a long time since I've seen a scene where citizens were so divided and arguing."

"I've heard that the atmosphere is that way right now. What is your position? Is it the same as that of the Truth Alliance?"

Gartrail laughed. It sounded like a human laugh, full of humor and empathy. But at the same time, it held a note of ridicule. "I don't know yet, but I'm not affiliated with the Truth Alliance. In fact, I might be the opposite. I understand your position and I agree with you. Joshua Kwon, I support you."

Joshua had a strange feeling. But there was no time to ask any more questions. He had to go to court.

"Go quickly, Joshua," said Gartrail. "I'll follow you."

Joshua said goodbye to Gartrail and headed inside the building.

A heavy silence fell among the hundreds of Diutin deputies, seated or standing on the small circular podiums floating around the courthouse. The second trial had begun, but it seemed no one wanted to break the silence. A gloomy, low, and dark atmosphere filled the room.

Suddenly, a figure in a dark blue robe stood up. It was Aureus.

"I am Aureus, a member of the Truth Alliance. I think all the lawmakers gathered here are aware of it, but Joshua Kwon, a human who is also a criminal, doesn't make sense."

The eyes of the lawmakers turned to Aureus.

"The point of his call for a double prosecution is to hold the Adola government accountable for the genocide, but those in charge of the Adola government at that time are already disappearing. Also, our people have not inherited the spirit of the government at that time. Of course, to borrow their terminology, they did not formally establish diplomatic ties with the humans of the world called the Desirée system ten years ago. I want to ask the lawmakers here whether we should establish diplomatic ties with them first in order to compensate them."

Members of the courtroom roared. Some nodded and some exchanged opinions with fellow lawmakers sitting next to them. Joshua saw Gartrail sitting down, silently watching the process, just like during the first trial.

"Even if you don't say it so zealously, we already know how much effort the members of the Truth Alliance have put into normalizing the old government, Aureus," said a visibly older alien. He was smaller than the other members of the council, but he was stout as if he was overflowing with power. His respiratory organs, visible through a small hole in his forehead, had become smaller as if they had lost their function, but his eyes were clear.

Aureus lowered his right arm and bowed his head in respect to the old Diutinian. "The same goes for the Sword of Light, Senator Brahra. What I'm trying to say is whether it's the Truth Alliance, the Sword of Light, or the members of the other Galactic councils speaking on this matter, the law applies the same." He pointed to where Joshua and Cassie were sitting. "They don't deserve to hold us accountable, because they're not Yudians."

"That seems to be in line with what Belaos said about the Caleb race, Aureus."

As Senator Brahra spoke, Aureus flinched.

"Belaos?"

Joshua and Cassie exchanged confused glances. They

didn't know what these aliens were talking about.

Senator Diane, who was on the other side of Aureus, said accusingly, "Senator Brahra, don't you know that talking about him is taboo?"

"I know, Diane. But why is it taboo? The story of that time is closely related to this trial. Even though he fell, isn't it true that remnants of his followers are still hiding somewhere in the galaxy?"

"They have no effect on us anymore, Senator. It's okay to talk about them, but why do we have to connect this with this trial? It's true that our leader, Varouar, joined them. But, didn't you mace him and his minions in the manner of our people? Aren't we here for something more than to reconvict the sins and transgressions of the past?"

"Or is it that the members of the Truth Alliance do not want to face the mistakes of the past? Is that why you made such stories taboo in our society?"

Diane appeared shocked at Senator Brahra's blunt words. "That's overly aggressive, Senator."

"Come on, let's settle down, Senators and get back to the matter at hand." Moderator Dunas, who had been watching silently, intervened. " Hypkeranos, the accused of the first trial, if you have anything to say, please do."

"Thank you, Moderator." Hypkeranos cleared his throat. "As Joshua Kwon said, in calling for a second prosecution in this second trial, we have a clear responsibility for our people. Actions come with consequences and responsibilities. It is true that the Diutinin warriors killed the humans of planet Han. And it is also true that we are responsible for it. The fact that everyone here wants to turn away from the truth is that we were being manipulated by the forces of darkness, and the events of that time are a past that we do not want to record in the glorious history of our race.

"And the members of the Truth Alliance worked hard for the government at the time, and thanks to that, we were able to quickly correct our mistakes and normalize the government. But wasn't Varouar a candidate for the Alliance of Truth? Also, aren't there legislators here who knew that Baruar was evil at the time, but ignored it and followed his instructions?"

Someone stood up and cried, "Shut up, Hypkeranos! It would be good for the accused to remember why he's here!"

Joshua frowned.

Cassie smirked and looked at him. "Connected intelligence? A harmonious society without conflicts?"

"Certainly, it's a rare sight from what we've seen of these aliens so far."

The courtroom was in chaos. Each of them started talking without getting a say, and in an instant, there was a commotion.

Dunas raised his voice. "Stop it right now before we put some of the councilmembers in custody!"

Still, the commotion did not subside easily.

Dunas snapped his fingers. Then, the discus of the two members of the Truth Alliance, who had been making a lot of noise, disappeared, and a glass tube came down and blocked them.

Gradually, the members quieted down.

Dunas looked disgruntled as he called out, "Let's take a break. The trial will resume in two hours."

During the break, Joshua, Cassie, and Hypkeranos gathered in the common room outside the courthouse. Guards stood outside the room to keep anyone from leaving.

"What does 'Yudian' mean?" asked Joshua.

"Your people call themselves humans, yes? It means something similar to that. We call ourselves Yudians," said Hyp.

"From what I hear in the courtroom, it seems like we've thrown a lot of controversy into your peaceful world."

"Very much so, Joshua. A very big controversy. You have ruined our quiet society. This trial is a huge issue outside of the courthouse. All the Yudians are talking about it."

"Do you know a congressman named Gartrail?"

"Gartrail? How do you know him? He is the chief councilor of the planet Nanat and the leader of a group called Selim's Followers."

"Selim?"

"It's almost like the Mother of Civilization. The selims they serve are a bit more primitive. That's why some members of the legislature reject them. They've actually fought civil wars with our people in historical times. They're gritty people."

"He says he supports me."

Hyp smiled bitterly. "Because he and Nanat's Yudians have also been rejected a lot by their own people as heretics. Joshua, it's not just Gartrail. Our society is suffering from this trial. But I personally think we should have been like this before. Yes, you should expose your secrets and overcome them instead of hiding them."

"You're getting over it? It seems like the confusion is only getting bigger and bigger."

"We will get over it, I believe."

"Is Moderator Dunas a neutral judge?"

"I don't know what you think of Dunas, but at least by our standards, he is a very progressive person. He is a

Yudian who always has a playful and challenging disposition when it comes to system-centric logic and established discipline. This trial could be quite interesting because of that."

"It's a problem because you've touched the facts that our society has made taboo and decided to forget," said another voice.

Joshua and Cassie got up and turned around. An alien appeared at the entrance to the break room.

Hyp called his name. "Victoranus."

"Hello, Hypkeranos, and humans. We are on opposite sides in the courtroom, but can we still talk?"

"What's going on, Senator?"

"I think it will be difficult to hide the truth from these humans any longer. We were both privy to what happened at the time, right, Hypkeranos? The superior ordered the massacre, but we actually carried it out. Before we go back into the trial, shouldn't we talk about the forces that took control of our government?"

Hypkeranos was speechless.

"Has Hypkeranos told you anything?" asked Victoranus.

"What are you talking about, Senator?" asked Joshua.

"About Propanus."

"I beg your pardon?"

"You really don't know. Propanus, the group behind Baruar, who ran our government at the time." Victoranus shrugged.

Getting annoyed at his vague words, Joshua stood up from his chair.

"Would you like to hear what I have to say or not, human?" asked Victoranus.

Cassie tapped Joshua on the shoulder. "I think we

should stay and listen to what he has to stay."

As Joshua reluctantly sat down again, Victoranus said, "Hyp, I think you'd better start talking first."

Hypkeranos looked at Victoranus once, sighed, and spoke to Joshua. "What do you want to know, friend?"

"What is this Propanus he just mentioned?"

The aliens' expressions turned clouded, and silence fell for a long moment.

"Are you curious about that, Joshua?" said Hypkeranos.

"Yeah. That would make the whole situation easier to understand. I think that's what your people have been trying to hide from us. What is Propanus?"

He looked around and said, "I suppose I can't hide this any longer, considering how I drove the members of the Alliance for Truth in the courtroom earlier. The point of this trial is to tell the truth of what happened ten years ago. Senator Victoranus, thank you. Thank you for this. Seeing that even I feel reluctant to tell this story, I must have been tainted by our society's taboos and customs, as well."

Victoranus nodded. "I think we'll get into that story as soon as the trial resumes. Because Dunas seems to be planning that."

"But one question is, why are you, who is on the side of the Truth Alliance, making such a proposal?"

Victoranus laughed. "I just figured the humans would find out sooner or later anyway."

Hypkeranus nodded at him. "Good."

"Hyp, what is Propanus?" asked Joshua.

"Do you have any guesses, Joshua?"

"Baruar, who was running the government of Adola at the time? I understand that he was part of Propanus. Hyp also said that unknown forces have run the government of Diutin. I know you don't want to talk about it, but I'm curious about their origins. Baruar is the word for a leader, like our 'President,' right?"

"It's a little different, Joshua. Baruar is a name and a proper noun, not a general noun for a leader. He was a little different from the president of your world, but let's call him a leader anyway. He was the leader of our race, elected by the people. He was a candidate for the Truth Alliance."

"Was he a part of Propanus? What is Propanus? Is it a group?"

"It means 'the ungodly.' It refers to those who are part of our race and who betrayed the Mother of Civilization." Hypkeranos had a sad expression on his face. "Our brothers and heretics we wanted to hide. They were the ones who caused the massacre on Planet Han."

"So, you're saying…their group took control of Diutin ten years ago in Adola system time, and they started a war?"

"Yes. When you brought up that fact and demanded a trial, you really brought up a history of shame that our people wanted to forget. Our people remember that time as a dark period of barbarism and violence. It is true that three ships from the Desirée reached our system, and it is true that one of the three, serving as a flagship, conveyed the meaning of the declaration of war to us in our language. We communicated that fact to the National Guard Corps Command. At that time, the command gave an order to attack. If you think of common sense, wouldn't it make sense for even the most reckless people to appear in the motherland of a different race with three ships and wage a fight?"

Victoranus made an uncomfortable expression for the

first time. "Soldiers cannot disobey orders. It was natural, Hypkeranos. The human race broke the intergalactic warp protocol and declared war against us. No matter how questionable the situation, I had to make a decision. I did. Command did too."

"Senator, I'm not blaming you. I'm just stating the facts. Joshua, those who ran our government at the time must have thought it was a good opportunity. I certainly objected to the directive, but my objection was dismissed. Anyway, we went to planet Han in pursuit of the ships you humans just launched."

"He was the Captain at the time, and I was the Vice Captain. I felt something strange when I arrived on the planet Han. We had already defeated two ships and led hundreds of ships into your world in pursuit of the last remaining ship, the *Incheon*, but the human race's air defenses were too weak and not well prepared for war. It was clear at a glance that you humans were bewildered. It was then that I knew something strange was going on.

"I asked Adola Command and Baruar to reconsider their orders. But the command insisted we carry on with the bombardment of the planet. We had already been subject to a declaration of war, and they said we must strike first before a militant heterogeneous race that disturbed the order of the universe would emerge."

Victoranus said, "The command gave us the order to attack, and I eventually followed it. It was only later revealed that our government officials were Proditor's minions."

"Proditor?" repeated Joshua.

"Proditor the ungodly," said Hypkeranos. "He is the one who created Propanus. The great leader who once made new homes for our race and ruled over the stars in the era of the great cosmos, the pride of our race. But now a heretic. The planet destroyer, the slayer, the seed of discord and war. Those are other names we call him."

Cassie's eyes widened. "I've heard that name! Joshua, remember? Dayweo told me about a flower called compel."

A tingling sensation ran through Joshua's head and into his stomach. "A long time ago, the Proditor who betrayed the Diutin society?"

"Did Dayweo tell you about him?" asked Hypkeranos.

"Just in passing." Joshua tilted his head. "But there's something I don't quite understand. Dayweo told the story as if it was a long time ago when the flowers were planted. Of course, we may have misunderstood. It was relatively recent?"

"No. You're right, Joshua Kwon. Proditor has been around for a thousand years."

"What do you mean? You mean two thousand years of human age?"

"Yes," said Victoranus.

"How is that possible?"

"Proditor is an immortal being. He used the dark energy of the universe to prolong his life. The Mother of Civilization that created our race was the right hand. It informs the energies of life and creation, and the universe circulates in conformity with nature. But Proditor found his own power in the ruins of the universe, and he learned how to take the life force of others and turn it into energy and use it to extend his life. Not the right hand, but the power behind the left hand."

Victoran continued to speak, "And those who follow him worship that power. They gave orders to take over our government and take our lives. We've been fighting Propanus for over a thousand years."

This was all too much for Joshua to take in. His mind was racing, and he didn't know what question to ask next.

Victoranus said in a subdued voice, "Those who have fallen into the dark side of the universe, we no longer see as Yudians. They are beasts. They are only destroyers. They have violated the teachings of the Mother of Civilization. We identify them by the symbol they worship."

He turned his left hand over and showed the back of it.

"They are the Worshippers of the Left Hand."

7.

Thirteen thousand years ago in Diutin's time and 2,600 years ago in human time, the Diutin race ushered in the era of the Great Space Age. The Diutinians were in the stage of advancing into the unknown parts of the universe that had been covered by a black curtain. At that time, Diutin society was still divided. It would be another five hundred years before society's connected intelligence took on a complete form.

Divided into dozens of factions and states, the Diutinians did not fully cooperate with each other. A small civil war began, but it did not escalate into a large-scale war. This is because, like humans, the Diutin people had experienced several devastating wars in the course of their historical development.

A Diutinian named Bellatrias lived during this time. He was born and raised in the Yud country on the planet Adola. He started his career as a member of the Assault Squad, the lowest level of Diutin warriors, and played a major role in the small civil war between Diutin countries with his outstanding skills. He gradually became the commander of Yud, and was finally elected as the leader of the whole planet. During his reign, Bellatrias united Adola. The civil war ended. The colonies within the system also submitted to the newly established unified planetary government of Adola.

He took the name of the country of Diutina, the Mother of Civilization believed by all Yudians, and changed it to Diutin. It was the birth of a unified Diutin people.

The Great Era began, and under the command of Bellatrias, the Diutin fleet left the Adola system and began to explore the outer systems of the galaxy. Planets with colonization potential were colonized with the help of Diutin's climatology, biology, and space engineering, and barren lands were pioneered as intermediate ports of call for the fleet. At its peak, they had civilizations on over sixty habitable planets, including in their own planetary system, and hundreds of interstellar ports of call.

Only then did Bellatrias stop expanding into the outside world and begin laying the groundwork for the world he had acquired. Yes, it was a world less than one-tenth the size of a galaxy, but the galaxy was larger than he'd expected, and the production capacity and population growth rate of the Diutin people was slower than expected. Also, his term was coming to an end. Even though he could've run again, Bellatrias resigned and stepped down without any regrets.

The Yudians mourned his retirement. But at the same time, they had high hopes for his only son, Belaos. Belaos was following the same path his father had taken. Like his father, Belaos left a great mark on the Diutin society and was growing as a leader.

Young Belaos discovered a civilized society of intelligence beings on the second planet of a planetary system with a red giant. The Diutinians were the first heterogeneous race these beings had encountered in the outside world. Belaos learned that the race, much smaller than themselves, had developed a mysterious and unique technology.

The technology these beings used to sustain their civilization, which they called "Caleb," was the dark energy that was widespread in the universe.

"Dark energy?" said Joshua, listening to Victoranus's story. "The matter and energy that's pervasive throughout the universe but cannot be comprehended?"

Hypkeranos nodded. "Yes, Joshua. That's it."

"These beings used it as an energy source? Does such a technology exist?"

"It does exist. But it's a dangerous technology, because the dark energy of the universe is the conduit that leads to the destruction of the universe."

"I don't understand."

"I will explain. When this universe was created, the universe created many elements and masses, and they became celestial bodies. But the parts that did not become empty masses and energy that seemed to be empty and nonexistent. This is what we call dark energy. It accounts for more than 90 percent of the universe. Our physicists and cosmologists believe that this dark energy gradually spreads through the universe, eventually destroying the rest of the energy and mass, and emptying the infinite darkness and stillness of the universe."

Cassie's brow creased. "But how can anyone use that energy? Humans also believe that there is something between the gravitational force and the masses of this universe, and that there are things different from matter as we know it. We also call it dark matter, or dark energy."

"Perhaps that's one of the few instances where two different civilizations give the same name to a simple and elusive fact, Miss Ice. But it does exist."

"Belaos learned that the beings created vast amounts of energy from small, trace dark energy," continued Victoranus. "In his view, it was a technology that could change the history of the Diutin race. After all, 99 percent of the matter in the universe is dark energy, so it was an infinite energy source. So, he wanted to communicate with the Calebs. He met with their race and discussed direct communication, and they sent a delegation to Mother Adola. Now, we've met several different races since then, but it was exciting for our people at the time. It was our first interaction with an alien race. All the citizens praised Belaos, and the retired Belatrias was proud of his son.

"Belaos was thinking of uniting with the Calebs and using their powers to create the ultimate energy source. We would no longer be just a civilization that went beyond this planetary system and moves between star systems, but a civilization that could cross galaxies, even entire universes. He dreamed of taking a leap forward."

Joshua wore a look of disbelief. "Did the technology of the Calebs make that possible?"

Hypkeranos spoke on behalf of Victoranus. "Belaos believed so. He became friendly with them and explored the deep universe through the equipment and technology they lent him. In doing so, he studied the technology of the Calebs. Up to that point, he was a young warrior with a sound mind and a just heart."

"Then what happened?" asked Cassie.

"The political situation began to turn against him," said Victoranus. "The leadership position was vacant for a while after his father, Bellatrias, retired. So, Adola started looking for a new leader. The merchants who were leading the trade at the time formed a trade association. They insisted on proposing a new leader, and it was not Belaus, but a young Yudian named Zenius who they brought forward. Belaos could not accept that fact."

Belaos was deeply heartbroken. He had always thought that he would inherit the position from his father. It was his father who had united the divided races and given them a single identity, and it was Belaos who would pioneer the universe. In addition, his reputation within the people was not comparable to anyone else. He assumed a group had rebelled while he was busy with the Calebs.

Belaos thought there was still room for negotiations. He stopped pioneering and returned to Adola after ordering Caleb's sympathizers and his subordinates to stand by.

On Adola, Belaos met the young Zenius, who had just been elected as leader, and the members of the council. They treated him with the utmost respect. Belaos calmly suppressed the questions that arose in his mind and talked with Zenius.

It wasn't long before Belaos learned that Zenius was a man worthy of being the Diutinian leader. Although he came from a powerful family of Adola, he was humble, and he had a deep interest and knowledge in commerce, politics, and technology. Belaos had to admit that the trade union members and the rest of the councilors had found the right person of good character. Although Zenius was younger than him, Belaos had a crush on him. Zenius promised to continue unparalleled support for the exploration of outer space, cooperation with the Calebs, and technology research on which Belaos depended. It would come with the active support of Adola civil society, Zenius said.

So, Belaos gave up his fight, forgot about his hometown, and returned to the Calebs.

He knew Adola was not a monarchy. Even his father, Bellatrias, had always said that the next leader had to be elected. Belaos wanted to earn the loyalty of the Diutinians through his pioneering work and create a world that would follow him. He wanted a world with a slightly more tilted weight toward him, not Zenius. Belaos did not yet realize that his desire would become a great ember later.

From then on, Belaos became more focused on the technology research of the Calebs. He wanted the Calebs he'd made a pact with to teach him how to access the heart of dark energy technology. But the Calebs would not do it. The Calebs knew of Belaos's desperate desire for knowledge—and power—and warned him. They told him that the "world beyond the veil" was not permitted to be accessed by the beings that currently made up the physical world of the universe, and if he tried to use the dark energy for such a thing, it would become a force that would cause the universe to lose its balance. But Belaos did not heed their warning. He continued his research independently.

Meanwhile, the Adola government and the council had found that a part of the world they'd taken over was brimming with discord. The frontier planets were attacked by unknown forces and devastated frequently. After discussion with Zenius, the council decided to send a group of warriors to the frontiers. Zenius accepted the resolution and issued an executive order.

They appointed Amanti as the commander of the detachment. Amanti, who was Belaos's lover, was Diutin's best swordsman. Armed with an intangible sword of photon waves moving with telekinetic power, she was dispatched to the frontier planet, Ulatos.

Amanti discovered on Ulatos that Caleb's army, which she had never seen before, had taken control of the planet. She requested reinforcements, but was quickly surrounded by Caleb's fleet.

Amanti had to buy time for aids to arrive. She made a decision. To make time for herself and the warriors who follow her, she led the assault ship she commanded into an asteroid belt near Ulatos. The Caleb fleet pursued them, but they could not move freely within the asteroid belt. That was what Amanti had been aiming for. She charged her flagship into the nearest cruiser. Amanti and the warriors pushed into the enemy ships and slaughtered Caleb's raid with photon swords. The absence of telekinesis powers in Caleb also eased their burden. By finishing one ship and then charging the other, Amanti took more than five of Caleb's ships out of control. And around that time, the aids of the colonial planet led by Adola's Central Army and Belaos arrived on the battlefield.

The war lasted twenty days. It was Diutin who won the victory.

"After the battle, the Diutin Council was convened,"

continued Hypkeranos. "Belaos blamed himself for not understanding the Caleb's intentions while he was working hard on the frontier. Everyone comforted him that it wasn't his fault. Anyway, he had been instrumental in helping Amanti defeat the Caleb army. Belaos told the council that he had been leading the exchanges with the Calebs, but they were not Yudians like us. He said that they shouldn't be treated like us. The leaders of our tribe did not question him much at the time. Belaos's words held a lot of persuasive power, and in the end, as he insisted, an expeditionary force was formed for war, and fleets were requisitioned from 100 planets.

"Naturally, the general leading the force was Belaos. There was no one to stop him. His lover, Amanti, stood by his side."

Hypkeranos smiled bitterly. At least, Cassie judged that it was a bitter smile on his face.

"There were many heroic battles and defeats, but in the end our people won the war. The war lasted over twenty years. Many colonies were destroyed. The scale of the war was so vast that over twenty billion Diutin lives were sacrificed, and Caleb was almost annihilated.

"The number of Calebs was far smaller than ours, but their technology was overwhelming. The engagement ratio was almost five to one. In the end, though, the Calebs were defeated. Our world suffered a great blow, but the victory was still a victory, and the Yudians praised Belaos. His political position was elevated to the level it was at before the rise of Zenius. And Belaus was elected leader when Zenius retired."

"The trial will resume shortly, so we'd better speed up the story, Vice-Captain," said Victoranus.

"Okay, Senator. The Adola Council soon realized that this terrible war had been organizedby Belaos."

"But how?" asked Cassie. "What happened to Caleb's army on Ulatos?"

"The Caleb army was made up of the same Calebs who followed Belaos. They had conquered Ulatos following Belaos's orders, and they were attacked by Diutin."

"What?" Cassie's mouth fell open. "He was behind all of it?"

Victoranus nodded. "Exactly."

Joshua shook his head. "Sacrificing your followers for your own political ambitions? How could he do such a thing?"

"He is a devil," said Hyp.

"Yeah, sounds like it. But why did Belaos suddenly do this? Was there a reason? There had to be a reason."

"Belaos realized that there was no way to uncover the secrets of Caleb's dark energy technology. That's why he waged a war. To get rid of the Calebs and find out their secrets. At first, I don't think he thought the war would escalate the way it did. It becomes clear when you read his records. But the war escalated and eventually led to the extinction of the Calebs. After the war, Belaos obtained as loot the archives and facilities that recorded most of their technology. He finally found out that he had been wrong. He discovered that the Calebs themselves did not know how to artificially create, control, and transform dark energy into useful energy.

"Still, Belaos could not abandon the possibility of dark energy. He was enraged that they hadn't told him the truth. But it wasn't over. He discovered the technology to generate dark energy in a way the Calebs forbid."

"What is that method?" asked Joshua.

"It was to transform dark energy into a catalyst for life energy. The converted energy was easy to handle, unlike other dark energies. It was forbidden knowledge," said Victoranus. "The most violent side of the universe was revealed by Belaos. It is the inverted left hand that symbolizes the forbidden power of the Calebs."

Following Victoranus's words, an image of the back of his hand turned upside down was projected into the air.

"The power of the left hand, which only the elders of Caleb possessed. The power of destruction and death. With that energy, a person can do anything. Even extend their lifespan. Belaos has become immortal. Hundreds of years after the extinction of Caleb, with all the energy sources available, Belaos sacrificed the citizens of Diutin to convert more life energy into dark energy. A civil war broke out. A civil war that lasted more than a thousand years. He disbanded the Merchant Coalition. The council was disbanded, and civil war broke out between the planets. The followers of Belaus were called 'Propanus', meaning 'the ungodly.' Belaos finally came to be called the Proditor. It means 'traitor.' It is of course our people that he betrayed."

Cassie sighed. "But how did the war end?"

"Diutin rose again from the wreckage of the war. Under the guidance of Bellatrias and Zenius, about twenty planets that had survived the war with Caleb formed a federation. It was the rebirth of the Diutin Federation. The two retired leaders led the army. They were the light in a dark time. Bellatrias mourned the fall of his son, but gathered the fleet and the remnant. Bellatrias and Zenius formed the Alliance of Truth. Their army crushed the forces of Propanus, but the battle was difficult nonetheless. It was

Amanti who made the war decisively swing to Diutin's favor.

"Proditor's lover, Diutin's strongest swordsman, Amanti, betrayed Proditor and Propanus and joined her people. In the final battle, Bellatrias, Zenius, and Amanti defeated Proditor's dark fleet and expelled him to the depths of space. Proditor was seriously wounded and disappeared. No one has seen him since. He was imprisoned in a place from which no one could escape. But for over a thousand years after that, the remnants of Propanus have plagued us. And ten years ago…"

"Did the crowd following him appear in Adola?" asked Cassie.

"Ten years ago, our leader, Baruar, wiped out all living things on the colonial planet," Hyp said, fiddling with his left hand, "and he attacked the humans of the Desirée system. He was a part of Propanus. And we fear Proditor himself will soon return."

Joshua didn't know what to say. Neither did Cassie.

"That's the truth," Hypkeranos said.

After a while, Joshua spoke in a quiet voice. "It seems that all Yudians are afraid of Proditor. That's why they consider this story taboo, forbidden."

Victoranus neither affirmed nor denied this. He didn't like Joshua's explanation. But it was also an undeniable fact.

Diutin society feared that Proditor would one day return.

"I see now, Joshua," said Hypkeranos. "The Worshippers of the Left Hand are everywhere. And they are still looking for opportunities in ways we won't expect. Those who hide in the shadows, waiting to fulfill the teachings of Proditor and fill the entire universe with dark energy.

There are people who sympathized with Propanus ten years ago sitting in the courtroom today. Because we couldn't condemn them, they ended up creating this situation. This trial is not just a place to discuss my sins. In addition to paying off our debt to Desirée humanity, it should be an opportunity to recognize and find the Worshippers of the Left Hand."

8.

The Diutin Council was a solid system that had lasted more than 2,000 years since the unified Diutin government was established. The first leader, Bellatrias, united the warlords and chiefs of the local nations of the planet Adola into a council. Later on, the leaders of the planets pioneered after the Great Space Age also became council members. The Alliance of Truth, which emerged as the central axis of Diutin society during the Ulatos War and the civil war with Belaos, declared that the council would decide on all political matters as a legislative branch and have other functions as well. The council became, in effect, the body that made all of Diutin's political decisions and even served as the judiciary. If the political system of mankind was separation of powers, Diutin's system had a structure of separation of interests between the executive and the judicial and legislative coalition, and one power. Such unity of powers made it possible to respond to war in a much more coordinated manner.

In other words, the war with Belaos, who became Proditor, was the direct cause of this political landscape.

For that reason, the weight of judgments and remarks of influential lawmakers belonging to the Truth Alliance was different.

When the trial resumed, Cassie's eyes seemed to see a little bit of the power composition of these Diutin councilors. Senator Brahra, a member of the Sword of Light faction, exerted great influence and won the respect of members of the Truth Alliance. However, other lawmakers spoke relatively little.

"We can keep saying the same thing," Brahra was saying now, "but the bottom line is that tens of thousands have died, and no one has been held accountable. And it was none other than our warriors, the watchmen of our civilization we trusted so much, who did it. Do you want to ignore this point? If there are entities that have not officially established diplomatic ties, do you mean that they are not treated in the same way as Yudians? Of course, bipartisan cooperation will be required, but the Alliance of Truth, which ran the former government and even supported Baruar, will have to take that obligation particularly seriously."

"The will of a lawmaker who thinks about justice is very noble, but Senator Brahra," replied Diane, fuming. "So, what do you mean? Do you mean we should apologize to the humans and then find and punish the councilmembers who backed Baruar? That doesn't even make sense!"

Tumultuous voices arose from among the Diutin people in the courtroom. When Joshua turned his head, he saw Aureus standing up from his seat.

"That's coercion! Our people also paid a lot of blood at

the time."

Concurring voices continued from the audience.

Someone spoke in a low but clear voice. "How is that coercion? I'm sure there was no proper apology and reparation. I agree with the prosecution, Joshua Kwon."

The court fell silent. A councilor stood up and looked around the members. It was a Gartrail.

Diane shouted at him. "Are you saying that as Selim and Nanat's representative, Gartrail? This is putting our people in limbo!"

"That's right! It was a confusing time and we are all responsible, but at the same time, we are all victims."

"Senator Brahra, a deputy must not drive our compatriots into chaos like this!"

Dunas raised his voice. "Please be quiet in the audience. Only the Yudians and humans who have a say in this trial should speak." Dunas shook his head, as if he was fed up with all of this, and called out to Joshua. "Prosecutor, please tell me your judgment on your prosecution and what you think should be the result. But, tell me only the gist."

"If I tell you what I think should happen, will it be done?"

"It will be taken under consideration, at least. But keep in mind, this is Diutin's courthouse. The judges, including myself, will make the decision. So, I encourage you to talk about everything carefully, but with no regrets."

"Okay, Moderator. I didn't know the full story of this case when it began, Senator Diane. But now I know what happened. Proditor's followers took control of the council and the administration of Diutin. They concealed their impure intentions and started a genocide. I don't fully understand how Diutin's leader Varouar was ousted at the time, and what was done to his minions, but it is clear that those who worked with the government back then were not punished. They should be punished. And they must also formally apologize and compensate the government of the planet Han. Until they are satisfied, and until the suffering is relieved, endless rewards and apologies must follow. That is my conclusion."

Giltarion shook his head. "Human Joshua Kwon, do you know how many of those responsible are here? In fact, most of the members of the Truth Alliance could be considered responsible, because most of them voted in favor of the attack on planet Han. That's all. Oh, and your friend Hypkeranos also cannot be freed from the accusation that he is a collaborator, because he commanded the fleet that attacked the planet Han together with Senator Victoranus. He apologized to you? You mean we should all go to jail? We were deceived. This mess has nothing to do with our sins."

"Senator, if I have any sins that need to be liquidated, I will accept the punishment as it is. And I will apologize to the humans," Hypkeranos said.

Giltarion shouted, "It's just a personal apology! You can't go against the will of our council! And before that, Vice-Captain, you must first be punished for giving away Diutin's assets to alien races without permission. That's obviously treason."

"That's not treason! Weren't you, the Alliance of Truth, the traitors who aided in the slaughter of different races, concealed and turned away the truth, and put shame on the face of the Mother of Civilization? Founders Bellatrias and Zenius will mourn in their graves when they hear what you have done."

"Please refrain from speaking, Vice-Captain." Giltarion waved his hand in anger.

Cassie whispered to Joshua, "It's the first time I've seen a Diutinian so angry."

"Me too, Cassie," he murmured back.

At that time, Victoranus, spoke for the first time since the trial reconvened. "Not all the words of Vice-Captain Hypkeranos are wrong."

Giltarion looked at him in disbelief. "Senator Victoranus?"

"Isn't it true that we were deceived by Propanus into doing something dishonorable? What would Belaos think if he saw this?"

"Belaos?" Senator Giltarion said as if shocked.

"You don't know Proditor Belaos? I'm sure he'd be very happy to see us arguing like this."

"He's dead!" said Diane. His voice was trembling. "What are you talking about, Victoranus?"

Brahra exclaimed, "Proditor isn't dead! He's still aiming for our world!"

Victoranus bowed his head toward Senator Brahra. "Thank you, Senator. Yes, he was kicked out of our world a thousand years ago. But don't you guys know? He wasn't dead."

"Yes, that's true Senator Victoranus," said Diane. "But it's been a thousand years. How could he possibly still be alive?"

"He extended his life with dark energy."

"That was then. No one has seen him since. Our ancestors sent him into exile in the heart of the galaxy. Our warriors scoured the galaxy and found his remnants and worshipers. But there was no evidence of him there. He must be dead."

"What do you think of what happened ten years ago? You don't think he had anything to do with that?"

"It can happen. Enough. There were many who believed in Proditor and wanted to do his will, even after the wicked one disappeared. But all of them were unsuccessful. Propanus can no longer threaten our people."

"You have proposed a resolution for special circumstances, including an attack on a planet."

Diane's mouth pinched at the sides. She said in a voice full of hostility, "Why are you talking about that?"

"Is that really what you meant?"

"What?"

"I'm asking whether you really judged the situation at the time and agreed to it independently. Isn't it strange? You were a biologist and historian who showed great interest in exchanges with different races. You spent a lot of time researching Calebs. I know you've been very interested in the human race, but why did you agree so easily to the slaughter of them?"

Diane stuttered with a shocked face. "I was just following my own theory. And the invasion of Adola by human race was a big, big event. You know what, Senator? It's been almost a thousand years since the war with Proditor. Isn't it rude to ask me such a question while following our party's argument?"

"Are you just following the party theory? If so, you are saying that the party theory of the Truth Alliance at the time was a war with different races. We also knew that if there was an actual war with humans, it would be catastrophic for them. It's not something everyone is unaware of."

Giltarion pointed a finger at Victoranus, accusing him. "You are the one who carried out that order yourself, Victoranus! Are you intimidating Senator Diane now?"

"Indeed, I was a coward, Senator. I am also responsible for the biggest part of this sin. Joshua Kwon, I can only say that my sin is great. But in the end, I obeyed the government's orders. In retrospect, it was the wrong order. Even if it was the command of my superiors, I should have rejected it. My second sin is that I realized it too late."

Joshua sat still, sensing Victoranus still had more to say.

"After the raid on the planet, everyone knew who Baruar was. I don't think anyone has forgotten who brought him down to the abyss."

"Victoranus, of course, I acknowledge your contribution, but..."

"Senator, I think we should acknowledge and compensate for the mistakes we have made against humans. And if you rely on that notion, the conclusion of this double trial is not that difficult. Wouldn't that make sense if you really think about it as an independent and individual subject?"

Victoranus looked around at the senators of Diutin. "Isn't that right, fellow lawmakers?"

Then he said to Dunas, "That will be all, Moderator."

Cassie whispered to Joshua, "Diutin's trials are really weird, Joshua. You talk whenever you want without stopping anyone, and now you tell the moderator that it's finished?

"Look at what nobody is saying, Cassie. I think Victoranus has a fairly large influence on the council. I didn't know what to think of him at first. He really is quite unpredictable."

"Even though he is one of those who slaughtered our

people."

"I know he is. Let's wait, Cassie, and see how this trial will end."

Dunas had a worried expression on his face. He slowly opened his mouth. "The first accused of the double trial is Hypkeranos, and the prosecution is the Alliance of Truth. And the second accused is the Truth Alliance, and the prosecution is the human Joshua Kwon. The two prosecutions are closely related, as they deal with war crimes, and it's becoming clear that the outcome of one will be the payoff of the other.

"It's not a criminal case, so we don't need proof. It is only the judgment of the facts that matters. In the end, only one conclusion is gradually popping into my head. It's scary to get this out of my mouth, but I'll tell you. In front of my respected lawmakers."

Dunas paused for a moment, then spoke quickly.

"We need to reveal who the followers of Propanus are and punish them appropriately. The conclusion is that we need to rediscover those who served as apostles of Belaos, and have since been hiding in the shadows."

In an instant, the hall went into an uproar. Meanwhile, Hypkeranos was nodding his head.

Dunas, noticing the agitation of the lawmakers and the audience, raised his voice in a stronger tone "Proditor and his apostles have always craved various forms of life. Their longing for dark energy has made them so. And, to the surprise of this court, some of the councilmembers gathered here today were once a part of that group. We have obtained various testimonies and witnesses that there are still people who are secretly acting as apostles of the shadows."

Joshua let out a long, anxious breath.

The room was soon in chaos. The legislators shouted. Members of the Truth Alliance raised their voices about the legitimacy of the trial, and some called Victoranus a traitor. Citizens who attended the trial were equally confused.

Victoranus raised his voice even more. "A month ago, the Durance colony was attacked, and our scientists in the lab were either killed or disappeared. Few people knew about the incident. My warriors and I followed their tracks. I found out that the fleet that attacked Durance wasn't just pirates."

Victoranus turned to Senator Diane. Joshua's heart was racing from all the excitement. He felt like he was watching a scene from a movie.

"Senator Diane, I think you are well aware of it. Because you were involved."

"What are you talking about, Victoranus?"

"The men you sent raided the Durance administration and burned the colony. You thought we didn't know? Now, tell me. Is Belaos alive? Where is he?"

Diane smiled with a pale face. "I don't know what you're talking about. I don't know why everyone keeps trying to intimidate each other. Isn't that right, Senator Brahra?"

Senator Brahra looked at Victoranus and then looked at Diane again. He repeated the action several times. It was obvious he didn't know what to do.

Giltarion opened his mouth with difficulty. "Victoranus…what the hell are you talking about?"

Victoranus did not take his eyes off Diane. "Warrior Dayweo will explain," he said softly.

A noise broke out in one corner of the courtroom, and

Dayweo and several other warriors appeared on their discs.

"My name is Dayweo. I'm a high-ranking warrior from the Adola Magistrates' Guard. This is an urgent matter. I want everyone here to listen! I have been dispatched here as an agent of the Adola administration. Remnants of Propanus have infiltrated the sanctuary guarded by the Mother of Civilization. They are believed to be from the same group that attacked Durance. Accordingly, starting today, the nodes of the connected intelligence in planet Adola will not run smoothly. This is a move taken by the Adola administration because of the fear of Propanus attacking Adola's connected intelligence nodes.

"There are people here in Congress who have been linked to those charges. Under the Constitution of the Diutin Federal Government, no non-arrest privilege applies to any case involving Propanus. In accordance with due process, the following members of the House of Representatives will be detained, and I declare that they will appear as the accused at the next trial."

Cassie gulped in her seat, her eyes wide. Joshua also knew that something urgent was going on. He clenched his fists.

"I'll keep this short. Members of the Alliance of Truth—Kaius, Hyiltra, Diane, and Giltarion. From the Sword of Light—Zerus, Calatras, and Gemonius. And from the Peace of Civilization—Jobius, Desirta, Kalium, and Omnius. The councilmembers of the Hart colony, and the councilmembers of the planet Jan, all of you are also named."

A transparent and smooth barrier lowered on the movable disk devices of each of the named members of the legislature.

The lawmakers screamed, and all kinds of remarks erupted in an instant.

"Stop it now!"

"By the Mother, this is an insult to Parliament!"

"Is it them?" Cassie said, trembling.

"I think so. They must be lawmakers who are accused of being with Propanus. But something is strange… This is too radical for the Diutinian way."

"Joshua, Hypkeranos is nervous."

Joshua looked at the defendant's seat. Hypkeranos said nothing, but he kept a close eye on what was going on.

"I don't think he knew this was going to happen. Was this all Victoranus's doing? He must have planned this from the beginning, Cassie."

Joshua looked at Victoranus, but because he was turned away, his expression was not visible.

Dunas solemnly declared, "The lawmakers will be detained until the next trial. Considering the complexity and seriousness of the case, we will make a decision at the final trial all at once. Therefore, this marks the conclusion of the second trial. Everyone is dismissed."

9.

Danny glanced at the edge of a long tower that seemed to stretch through the clouds and into space. From the middle of the tower and above, flying cars and hovercraft were constantly moving. Some of them rode long glass tubes into and out of the building. It was a more complex and well-designed tower than Danny had ever seen before.

This was the headquarters of Granot Group. The office building was located in the heart of Altra, the capital of New Shanghai. The massive crystal and spiral structure looked as if it had several metal arms. Danny and Aiden parked their A-wing in the basement of the office building, and waited in the reception room on the first floor.

"What do you think of this place, Danny?" asked Aiden.

Danny looked at Aiden. "How wealthy are the owners of this company? Are they paying taxes all the time?"

Aiden chuckled. "The money they make must be astronomical. They produce all of the social overhead capital and military equipment of the Union government.

All household appliances and high-tech products for the average household of ordinary citizens are also made here. Still." Aiden lowered his voice. "I heard that the corporate tax alone is 100 billion yuan per year."

Danny whistled. "100 billion yuan?" That number was a little less than 20 percent of the annual budget of the Union government.

"Captain Danny Carlos?" said a voice.

When Danny turned his head, he saw a female secretary with a slender body. "Yes?"

"I am Wang Fei, the boss's secretary. The boss is waiting for you in her office. I will take you there."

Danny and Aiden followed the secretary into the elevator. She pressed the 250th floor, and the door closed. The elevator zoomed up at an astonishing speed. Danny had barely counted to five when the elevator stopped and the door opened.

A woman stood by the window, waiting for them. Aiden and Danny glanced at each other, not sure what to say.

"Captain Carlos," said the woman. "Nice to meet you. My name is Yeoreum Granot."

"Hello, Ms. Granot," he replied. "I'm Captain Danny Carlos, commander of the Third Regiment of the Allied forces. It's a real honor to meet such a famous person. My friend here is Sergeant Aiden."

"Nice to meet you, Sergeant."

"I'm assuming you heard that we were coming."

Yeoreum Granot, the president of the Granot Group, grinned softly. "Yes. And if it's the Third Regiment, I'm well aware of it personally. The Third Regiment and the Mobile Squadron's munitions, ships, and gravity devices are all made by our company."

"At the moment, you are also making the best-performing handy tools on the market." Danny gestured to the handy tool on his arm.

Yeoreum laughed. "Thank you for the compliment. But that's not why you're here, so let's get straight to the point. What do you need from me? The chief of staff told me to get you anything you require."

"I would like to use one of your ships."

"What kind of ship? I'm confident that most of our ships have the features you want. From ion cannons, plasmas, rail cannons, to missile batteries. We have ships from small to large, and capable of long voyages. May I ask where your destination is?"

"Neptunus. I have to get there faster than anyone else, or at least as fast as them."

Yeoreum twisted her mouth. "If it's Neptunus, you will be able to reach it quickly enough on a ship with the existing specifications."

"I don't want an existing ship." Danny smiled. "I want a ship equipped with a wormhole generator. Do you have one? I heard there is a prototype made by Granot."

Yeoreum shrugged. "I'll admit, I hoped you wouldn't ask for that. It's still top secret. These are a few precious prototypes. It may take a little longer for mass production products to come out."

"Looks like that's the case," said Aiden.

Yeoreum looked at him, expressionless. "Indeed. Joshua Kwon, the enemy of the Union government, also owns an FTL ship, right?"

"FTL?"

"Faster than Light. Another name for our warp-drive technology."

"I know that term," said Danny. "It's believed that *Robespierre's* technology is not human, but alien technology. Crazy, huh? This is a personal question, but the warp-drive technology, is it the same technology the planet Han made twenty years ago?"

Yeoreum nodded. "The researchers working together with the Allied government's Scientific Research Institute are all our staff dispatched from Granot. And we've come to understand most of the planet Han's warp drive and wormhole creation technology."

"That's great. Then can you show us the prototype?"

Yeoreum opened the console in the center of her office. The red light on the console scanned her iris and turned on. After a while, a hologram appeared. It was clear that the artificial intelligence "G" was installed in all androids of Granot.

"What's going on?"

"Please connect Dr. Cheng."

A few moments later, a voice belonging to a middle-aged man was heard. "Yes, boss."

"Dr. Cheng, I'm bringing the guests to your department. Prepare *Soros I* and *Kudo*."

"Okay."

The communication ended.

"*Soros I*?" asked Danny.

"It's a tentative name. It's highly likely to be confirmed. The newly built warpable heavy cruiser will be the Soros class. And the assault ship will be the Kudo class."

"Kudo used to be the president of New Sydney and New Shanghai."

Yeoreum looked rather impressed. "That's right. Are you interested in history? You sound like a scholar."

Danny smiled. "What, you aren't used to someone so erudite?"

"There are a lot more ignorant people these days, Danny," said Aiden.

Danny and Aiden followed Yeoreum out of the office. They entered a high-speed elevator. After the doors closed, they began to descend at an alarming rate.

"Where are we going?" asked Aiden.

"It's on the 25th basement floor."

"Are the facilities packed so deep? It makes you wonder what kind of architectural engineering was mobilized."

"The whole tower runs on a twenty-four-hour decompression system. The building was designed to be resistant to all kinds of cosmic radiation damage and bombing. And some of the company's most secretive projects are underground, not above ground."

The elevator reached the 25th basement floor in ten seconds.

When the door opened, a skinny man with glasses and jeans stood there. "Boss, I have it ready. This way."

The group walked in the direction he was pointing. Gradually, the corridor widened, and the entrance to a large hall where light poured in appeared.

Danny saw the two smoothed-out cruisers and the assault ship shining through the dim shadows in the middle of the hall. T-I and K-I were engraved on the side of each ship's hull, respectively.

"Thank you, Doctor," said Yeoreum.

"Call me if you need help, boss."

He passed through the double door on the side of the hall.

After Danny and Aiden looked at each other for a moment, Yeoreum said, "You can choose any of them, Captain."

"Honestly, heavy cruisers are attractive to me, but for me and my regiments to be 100 percent functional, I think an assault ship with similar specs would make more sense."

"Are you talking about the Kudo class?"

"Yes. Can we handle the ship right away without special training?"

"The interface of the console will look familiar. Calculating coordinates during warp drive is a bit tricky, but if you specify a few cosmic random and imaginary numbers correctly, most of them can be calculated automatically by the navigation device. As long as you know basic physics and cosmic random numbers, it won't be a big deal."

"That's fortunate."

"And you should know, there is also a training room for the Union's telekinetic agents, Captain."

Danny's eyebrows rose in surprise. "In this little spaceship?"

"Let's just say it's a small favor for the hero," said Yeoreum with a smile.

Danny blushed. "I'm no hero."

"Yes, you are. If you hadn't been in Connecticut that day, the number of victims would have been much higher. No need to be humble. As a capable person, I am especially grateful."

Danny recalled the memory of hearing that Granot's successor possessed telekinetic powers. Aiden had told him, *She's super talented.*

"How did you get your powers, boss?" asked Aiden.

Yeoreum Granot's eyebrows furrowed slightly. "I'm

sorry. I don't want to answer that question. It's a personal matter."

"Aiden," said Danny, Giving him a warning look. It was clear by Yeoreum's expression that she didn't want to talk about the subject.

"Forgive me, Sergeant," she said. "When I see people with telekinetic abilities, I feel a strange sense of comraderie. We are neighbors that everyone looks down on and no one wants to get too close to. Being unwelcome is what I'm most used to in my life. It is also part of my true self-consciousness. I had to learn from a young age how to not show my feelings and not be seen by others. Of course, I still had a smoother life than those who are less capable than me. But that feeling of isolation…it lasts a long time. Captain, I'm sure you understand."

Danny nodded in agreement. "I understand, ma'am."

"I thought so." Yeoreum smiled softly and pointed to the *Kudo*. "Come in. I'll give you a quick tour."

Upon entering the cabin, an automatic sensor detected movement, and the lights came on. They passed through a long cylindrical passage into the control room. Danny thought it was a simplified design compared to the ships he had seen so far. In fact, even more so compared to the *Little Boy*, an assault ship of the same weight class. When he mentioned that, Yeoreum agreed.

"That's right. The control room is much more simplified than on conventional ships. The number of consoles has been cut in half. This is largely due to the latest warp-drive autopilot. So far, the console for calculations between the navigator and the system has been minimal. We needed one more, but now the autopilot can control just about anything."

"The engine is also different. It's a direct injection engine that explodes from the fusion cluster through the combustion chamber and power generator. It has a lot more power and stability. There is no need for agency personnel to manually check each power phase change or the nuclear silos. They are all controlled by the various shielded bulkhead internal systems. It's still a prototype, but it's a ship with breakthrough speed and durability."

"I'm looking forward to testing it out," said Danny, smiling. "Thank you again for lending it to us."

"Take care of it for me, Captain. It's a ship I really cherish," said Yeoreum. "Please treat it with kindness."

He wondered if she was joking a bit, but she wore a serious expression. She *must be a mechanical fanatic*, he thought with a slight smirk.

"I will, Ms. Granot." He tried to ignore the look Aidan was giving him in the background.

A little while later, as they flew the *Kudo* through the open top of the tower, Aidan said, "One thing is certain. This bastard is a beast, Danny."

"How's the power?"

"It's amazing. It takes a little over five seconds to reach top speed. Lu Xun is going to love it. He'll probably live in the engine room; I'd bet all my money on it."

"I'm sure you would." Danny chuckled. "Everyone will love it. Not to mention Kirox."

"Let's go pick them up, Captain."

Danny nodded. "Let's do it."

A button on the console beeped. A communication was coming in.

"Who is it?" asked Danny.

Aiden pressed the button to receive the communication.

A hologram of the President's chief of staff appeared. "Captain Carlos. This is Sura Handler."

Danny fought to hide his grimace. He put on a bright face. "Chief Handler, how are you?"

"Do you like the new ship?"

"I really like it. It has a power and performance I've never seen before."

"I'm glad to hear that. I'm going to give you a briefing." Sura Handler laughed at his play on words.

Danny was surprised that he could laugh. "Tell me what I need to know."

"You will go to Neptunus's secret research facility. As is known, there are no separate administrators there. There is only the director, Dr. Alice Heckerman."

"I see."

"I have informed the doctor that you will arrive shortly."

"Is she in charge of the entire lab?"

"It's hard to explain, but it's possible."

Danny wondered what that meant. "Okay."

"You just need to get there and capture Yuri Ivanova, and secure her recruits. That's it."

"Okay."

"Do you have any more questions?"

"No, Chief Handler."

"Then, good luck with your mission. Don't disappoint us." The chief of staff disappeared. Danny swallowed hard as a chill went down his spine.

Aiden shrugged. "Well, it seems like a simple mission, right?"

Danny wasn't so sure, but he nodded. "Call Kirox."

"Will do."

After a few moments, a hologram of Kirox appeared with a ringing tone. Kirox answered with a bored expression.

"When are you coming?"

"I'm on my way to the grounds on a new ship, Kirox. Where is Lu Xun?"

"He's sleeping. Shall I wake him up?"

"Yeah, I think I'll be there in ten minutes. Get ready to board with the rest of the crew."

"Okay. How was the girl?"

"Who?"

"Yeoreum Granot, boss. Is she as pretty as everyone says? I'll give you my contact information when I have time. Maybe you can pass it on to her."

Danny rolled his eyes. "Cut the bullshit. Do you think a woman like her wants *your* contact information? Quit the funny talk and get ready to work."

"Neptunus is full of bastards, Captain. Speaking of which, I don't really like this operation. It doesn't sound that fun."

"If you catch Yuri Ivanova, you will receive a special reward. Does that make it more fun?"

Kirox nodded, his eyes brightening. "Okay. See you soon, Captain."

The hologram vanished.

Danny sat back in the captain's chair with a sigh, falling into his thoughts for a moment. This mission should have been straightforward, yet…it wasn't.

Aiden's voice pulled him back to reality. "Are you thinking of her, Danny?"

"Yuri Ivanova?" Danny figured there was no point in pretending. "That's right. I was thinking of her."

"There's nothing wrong with it. I bet she's thinking of you, too. Cheer up, Danny."

"Shut up. Everyone has a lot to say today."

"I just care about you, Captain. That's all. I know what it's like to get your heart broken."

Danny ran a hand through his hair. "I don't know, Aiden. She lied to me. Damn, that woman was a Discarded, and she was a tycoon. What can I say when I see her again? Missed you? Came across the wormhole to meet you? She's my enemy now." He set his jaw. "And I'm going to get her."

Aiden laughed softly. "I'm sure you will, Captain."

Yeoreum followed the rear view of the ship as it flew through the top screen of her office. The ship's engine emitted a blue light from the exit and then moved away in an instant.

Dr. Cheng came in, but Summer didn't turn to him. Yeoreum shook her head and closed her eyes.

"They are so mean," she said. "They even sent Harry Carlos's grandson."

Without saying a word, Cheng took the wine out of the closet and poured it into a glass. As he held out the glass, Yeoreum accepted it and smiled.

"Thank you."

Cheng swallowed the wine down his throat. "Why did you reveal that you are capable, Yeoreum?"

Yeoreum emptied the wine glass and looked at Cheng Granot, the chairman of the Granot Group. "What else should I have done, Father?"

"Chief Handler and President Soros don't forget where we came from. Sending Danny Carlos is their signal to us.

Don't forget to obey."

"We've already given them a lot, right? What more can we do?"

"Everything…at least until they're gone."

"It will be soon, too." Summer laughed. "I'll have to prepare the ship again."

"Right." Dr. Cheng sighed.

"Captain, what are you thinking?"

Yuri looked at Junkou.

He shrugged. "You seem to have a lot of thoughts."

"Oh, sorry. Was I staring at you on accident?"

"It's okay to stare. May I ask what you're thinking?"

Yuri shook her head. "It doesn't matter."

"Usually when people make that kind of expression, it's something they don't really want to say, or they're thinking about someone important without realizing it. Which one is it, Captain?"

"Well…both of them make sense. Which one do you think it is?"

Junkou grinned. "Since you've been looking at me, maybe one of my colleagues? Are you thinking of my predecessor, Dallas?"

"I'm really sorry about what happened to him, but no. Oh my, I'm really sorry…I was thinking of you and Haneul."

"Oh, Haneul? What did she do?"

"On this mission, Junkou, if you make a mistake again and the worst happens, I'm afraid Haneul will blame me."

"Are there any better pilots besides me?"

"No."

"Then you made the best choice." He flashed a grin at

her. "Don't worry about me."

Yuri forced a smile and looked around. The *Puree* was a medium frigate belonging to the *Moscow* ship. They were heading toward Neptunus, set on an automatic course.

"It's not that I feel sad for her already. I just want my crew to be careful."

"One thing I can say is that we still have a long way to go. Were you unable to get some sleep before departure? Captain, get some sleep. There's still more than a day left until Neptunus."

"Yes, you're right, Junkou. I'll take a break and come back. Make sure you end your shift on time too."

"I will, don't worry."

Yuri left the control room. She returned to her little room, took off her uniform, and lay down for a while.

She looked at her beeping handy tool. A communication was arriving. She smiled and answered. A hologram of a woman with long hair and a tunic appeared above her palm.

Yuri spoke. "Sister."

Irina Ivanova grinned. "Where are you, Yuri?

"I can't tell you where. Someone might be eavesdropping. When will I be able to see you?"

"Yes. I want to meet you too, Yuri." Irina had a sad expression on her face.

"Sister, I've been thinking of some old memories recently. Like the villa Father took us to. Remember?"

"I do remember. You had nightmares."

Yuri's eyes lit up. "I think the creature in that dream is like Father."

"Yuri, you must be very sad."

Yuri rubbed her eyes. "Unnie, it's been so long since I've

seen you. It's been over ten years."

"I'll see you soon. Yuri. We'll see each other soon."

"How can you be sure?"

Irina's hologram reached out. "Yurina, I think someone's listening in. I'll turn off the communication."

"Wait, don't go," said Yuri.

"I'll call you back. I'll call you back soon. Take care of yourself."

"You too, sister."

Irina's hologram disappeared. Yuri thought for a moment in the dark.

She hadn't told Junkou earlier, but she'd also been thinking about Danny Carlos for a moment. And Karan Shetty.

And of her father, who had disappeared.

Yuri recalled the dying marine creatures she had seen in her childhood dreams.

IO.

As they approached the outer orbit of Neptunus, Yukyung saw the blue dot floating in outer space grow bigger and bigger. The blue dot exuded its own presence in the emptiness of space where far-off darkness and fear spread endlessly. The twin planet of New Sydney, covered with water, the sign of life. Underneath the paradise planet's atmosphere, a thick intrigue was looming and preparations were underway to welcome visitors.

Kamura's voice came from behind Yukyung. "It's a planet with strong gravity."

Yukyung turned and looked at Kamura. He was about to stab his railgun, Death, into the holster of his special combat suit.

"I know that the gravity is less than twice that of New Shanghai. So, if I set foot without a combat uniform, I'll quickly get tired. Right?" said Kamura darkly.

"Gravity won't be our biggest problem down there."

Yukyung thought of the corpse creature that had

swallowed Yeonwoo. The memory made her feel dizzy, but she managed to keep her bearings.

The time is coming.

She felt a chill wrapped around her body. It was a chill emanating from the depths of her soul.

An announcement from Junkou, who was in charge of piloting the ship, came over the loudspeaker.

"The *Puree* will enter Neptunus's atmosphere in under thirty minutes. We're wearing a cloak, but they'll soon know we've landed. We'll try to land ten kilometers east of the base in the Southern Hemisphere, and then go through the seabed to the dome. We'll approach it and use the excavator to secure the access to the underground."

Another voice came on. "This is Yuri Ivanova. After that, the ground troops, including Captain Kamura, and the Brotherhood will take charge of the entry. Everyone else, please wait in the rear, including Junkou. In case of emergency, you must wait at a distance to secure an escape route. We will not exceed two hours. If that time approaches, we will retreat to the main ship, no matter the outcome."

A tense atmosphere filled the ship.

Yuri finished speaking. "Then let's go."

Concealed by the cloak, the *Puree* reached the Sea of Neptune safely after a twenty-minute flight. Yuri admired the sight that appeared briefly through the screen. The sea and the glimmer of light cast a reddish hue across the planet. But soon the sight disappeared, and as the *Puree* descended rapidly, the landscape darkened under the sea. The decompression device in the cabin of the *Puree* started to work, and a noise began. It was one of the devices meant to sustain the life activities of the crew.

Soon the *Puree* reached the roots of the man-made structure where the dome was located. The roots were combined with metal compounds and rocks, and the ship's geological analyzer indicated that it was part of the skeleton of a structure designed to withstand various corrosive forces.

The front snout of the *Puree* protruded forward. The snout soon turned into a cone like a drilling rig, and began to carefully pierce the sides of the structure.

The crew waiting inside the airlock heard Junkou's voice. "This is harder than I thought. It's going to take some time. I'll increase the output."

Kamura could sense the slight uneasiness in the voice of the pilot.

"Are you afraid, Kamura?" asked Karan.

Kamura shook his head. "At this age, I don't fear anything, pirate. I'm just a bit reluctant. I think it's because of what Desmond said, but there are definitely ominous things we don't know about here. I don't like the smell of that insecurity. It's a gloomy feeling."

"It's ironic that such a dog thing is happening to Neptunus."

"What's ironic?"

"Neptunus is like a dream in Valhalla. Valhalla is a barren breed, home of ghosts. Even now, the people of Valhalla hear their voices at night. I too grew up hearing them. Wind and earth made them. The voices and footsteps of the ghosts of death. New Sydney's great ocean and green land were the object of envy, a symbol of all the absurd and unfair possessions enjoyed by those who expelled us. It was an unacceptable riot that the universe wielded against us to create an oceanic planet in our system, rich in vitality. Looking at the two seas not far away, in comparison to our planet's dry land and few seas… When you see the sea, you'll understand."

Kamura didn't doubt him. He knew too well how the deprived felt.

Karan continued, "I sometimes wonder why the one-armed Balthazar didn't settle here. I guess because he didn't have the manpower or technology to do so at the time. But everyone knows that Balthazar Mayer was always thinking about acquiring New Sydney and Neptunus during his lifetime. For the residents of Valhalla, this place used to be considered a paradise.

"But the Union didn't see it that way. No, they thought of this place only as a factory for secret experiments and conspiracies. I knew the Alliance is run by horrible people, but what they did here is particularly upsetting. Isn't that right, Desmond?"

"I am not an idealist or a philanthropist, but the Union must be punished for what they have done to this system," said Desmond, his eyes narrowed.

"Do your old colleagues feel the same way?"

"Of course not. Many of them refuse to question the government and faithfully follow the government's propaganda. But there are others like me. If enough of them see, then we could really build an army to take down the Union."

Yukyung snorted. "That's not going to happen."

Everyone's attention focused on her.

"What are you talking about?" said Desmond, with a displeased look on his face.

Yukyung, who had been looking at the floor, raised her

eyes and looked around the room. A smirk tugged at her mouth.

"They don't think of humans as humans. Haven't you all seen the genocide Amon Soros and Sura Handler unilaterally committed on Han and Valhalla? They manage the army effectively. Unrest within the military has never happened since the President took office. Desmond, you're the only exception."

"So, what, you don't believe this revolution will succeed?" asked Jena.

"No, I can't say I do. I've seen things and learned things that none of you understand. Do you know why I'm here? I'm here to die, swallowed by a greater darkness. It almost happened once before. You'll soon understand what I'm talking about."

"That's not right."

The access door of the airlock opened, and Yuri entered. She spoke firmly to the audience.

"We didn't come here to die. We came here to make the revolution a success. Yukyung, I know it must be difficult to come back here. To be honest, it's hard to fathom how hard it must feel. But we didn't come here to give up. We came here to uncover the secrets of the Union, and to prevent the misfortunes of the planets Han and Valhalla from happening again. So, please don't say that you're going to die." Yuri looked from Yukyung to the others. "I don't want any of you to think like that. If we die, we're giving the Union what they want."

Those gathered there murmured in low voices to signify their agreement. Karan smiled and nodded to Yuri.

Yukyung shook her head. "Captain Ivanova, you will soon find out."

Without further ado, she put on a combat helmet. Yuri didn't answer.

The airlock opened, and Yuri and thirty other crewmembers quickly disembarked from the ship wearing combat uniforms. As soon as she came out of the first entrance, Yuri saw several bulkheads. She opened a comm link and asked Junkou, "Where are we?"

"At the bottom of the dome," he answered. "Based on my scans, there should be an elevator that goes up to the upper floor 200 meters ahead. I don't know how far it goes."

"Okay."

The group moved toward the front right of the ship, along the slanted road. After a while, the elevator that Junkou was talking about appeared. The elevator was huge and could accommodate twenty people at the same time.

"We'll go up first," said Yuri. "Kamura, follow along with the land crew."

Kamura nodded.

Yuri got on the elevator first. She noticed that it would only take them deeper underground. Considering that their current location was under the sea, she'd hoped this elevator would provide an exit to the seabed. But there wasn't another obvious route to take. The elevator carrying the first group, which consisted of Yuri and most of the Brotherhood, moved toward the basement.

"What were they doing hiding in such a dark place on Neptunus like mole rats?" said Karan.

"We'll find out soon."

"My intuition is telling me, Yuri, that this whole operation is really dog shit."

The elevator reached the basement at high speed. The heavy doors opened. The light installed in the visor of their combat uniform turned on as they stepped forward into near-darkness. Faint lights from the ceiling dimly illuminated glass tubes around the basement. It looked like a huge hall.

Karan pulled out his plasma cutter, muttering, "Damn, what is all this?"

Inside the glass tubes, they could barely make out silhouettes that looked like human limbs, as well as figures that looked like quadrupeds and sea creatures.

"Are these people?" Jena ran closer to the glass tubes. "There's something strange about them, boss."

Karan scanned the glass tubes one by one. "What the hell is this?"

Just as Yuri was about to say something, Yukyung's voice came through the crew's visors.

"They're not humans. What you're seeing are aliens."

"Alien?" said Karan.

Yuri put her hand on one of the glass tubes and read the description underneath it. She moved on to another and did the same "There are symbolic names, the date and duration of the experiment, and the condition of the subject... I don't think these are humans or Diutinians..."

"Yeah, their heads are too strange, and the length of the limbs and the structural arrangement and proportions of the body are clearly different," said Jena. "If Diutinians and humans are a little closer to mammals, these feel more like amphibians or reptiles. Look at this one—it's got four eyes." He pointed to one of the glass cages. "What the hell are these creatures?"

"These are the Calebs," said Yukyung.

"Caleb?" Karan frowned. "Is there such a race in our galaxy? Are there other races besides the Diutinians and humans?"

"They are an ancient race. A little older than the Diutinians. Diutin discovered them. They were an advanced race. Although, as you can see, they are now prisoners of the Union."

The elevator doors opened again. Yuri glanced over her shoulder to see Kamura and the land combatants appearing from behind.

"I heard what you all were saying," he said. "Are you sure they are a new race?"

"According to Yukyung, they are."

"Everyone, come this way!" Jena called the others.

He pointed to a console panel at the end of the bulkheads. When Yuri got closer and looked at it, she saw unknown patterns drawn on the panel. The grids were convex to form a geometric shape. A big button lay at the center of the shape.

"Shall we press it, Captain?" Jena asked.

Karan nodded, though he looked uncertain.

"Wait, don't—!" Kamura reached out to stop Jena, but he had already pressed the button.

A fierce vibration ran through the hall's floor, and the bulkheads shifted, forming a passage between them. The whole structure of the hall had changed.

"Damn it. This place is a maze!"

The glass tubes and alien figures had disappeared. The console panel had also disappeared. In addition, two forks appeared in front of them, leading in two different directions.

Yuri thought fast. "Let's divide into two groups and split

up to investigate what else is in this place," she said.

Kamura agreed. "That sounds like a good plan."

"There doesn't seem to be any jamming fields or EMPs, so communication should be possible," said Jena.

Yuri nodded. "The land squadron and I will take the left fork, and the Brotherhood can take the right one. If anyone finds something, let the other group know right away."

"Will do, boss," Karan said to Yuri, but he seemed reluctant to leave her. "You be careful, Yuri," he added.

Yuri went forward with Kamura and the land squad members. She called Junkou through her comm link.

"Yes, Captain?" he replied.

"Continue scanning our location, Junkou. We just split into two groups, the army squadron and the Brotherhood. Keep an eye on where we're going."

"Why did you split up?"

"Jena touched a device, and it completely changed the structure of the hall."

"Do you think it's a trap?"

Yuri swallowed hard. "I don't know yet."

"Okay. I'll keep an eye on you."

The path continued in a straight line for about twenty minutes. When they came to another fork, Kamura said, "Let's go to the right."

"How do you know, Kamura?"

"If you listen hard, you can hear footsteps in that direction. I think the pirates are close. And since the right path looks more worn, it seems to be a road that people frequent."

"Okay, right it is then," said Yuri.

As they continued on, she noticed something on the wall, which was made of unknown metal. Geometric lines were drawn on part of it, along with a human figure.

Kamura spoke as if he had guessed what she was thinking. "That doesn't look like it was drawn by a human."

"What, you think an alien drew it?"

"It seems so, but it's hard to be sure."

"Was this place made by aliens?"

"It could be. What I don't understand is why their story isn't being told anywhere. It would be arrogant to say that the Diutin and humans are the only intelligent beings in this universe. But somehow, we have overlooked these beings. It's hard to believe. Maybe their race went extinct a long time ago."

Yuri felt the same way. Her heart raced as she wondered how long the Union had known these secrets, and what else they were hiding.

"Yukyung, tell me more about what you know," said Yuri. "About those creatures called Calebs."

"What are you curious about, Captain?" asked Yukyung.

"Since we don't have much time, let's assume what you said. These are probably intelligent, bipedal creatures like us and the Diutinians, and, according to you, they are older than Diutin. Why are they here in those cages? Is it a matter of only those individuals, or is it the common fate of all Calebs?"

Everyone's attention was focused on Yukyung.

"They lost the war against Diutin," she said. "It was a long time ago. By the time humanity was just moving from Mother Earth to prehistoric times, the Diutinians were already colonizing the surrounding systems. The Caleb tribe was on another planet they found during their colonization. The Calebs were a presbytery race. They stopped expanding and tried to retreat. But they made a mistake and were attracted to a strong Diutinian—the leader of Diutin, Belaos."

Yuri made a puzzled expression. "How the hell do you know all that?"

Yukyung smiled in a way that sent a shiver down Yuri's spine.

Kamura thought she seemed different than before. *Something strange is going on here.*

"Follow me," said Yukyung. "I'll show you what I found, Captain."

Karan found a gigantic circular laboratory filled with rows of coffins. Desmond glanced over the central console panels.

"Can you analyze it, Desmond?" asked Jena. They didn't want to make another mistake in pressing a button and mess up the maze again.

"It's possible, Jena. All the systems here follow the Allied protocol. Security is also made up of codes I know."

"How much time do you need?" asked Karan.

"Give me ten minutes."

Karan nodded. Desmond started working. Bypassing the Allied security system, he began to build an access road.

Jena looked around the dim coffins. He narrowed his eyes, noticing that there were whitish figures in the coffins. "Do you all see those?" he said.

"Are these the same aliens we saw earlier?" asked Karan, moving closer to inspect them.

"I don't know," said Jena. "But they must live a lonely existence, stuck as a lab rat in this corner of the universe, while no one else has any idea they're here."

"'The total amount of misfortune is limitless,'" said Karan, quoting the words of an admiral from long ago, during the planet pioneering era. "The bottom of unhappiness is so deep that no one can fathom it. Let us mourn their fate."

Jena walked around and tapped the coffins. A thumping sound rang out.

"These tubes appear to be connected to that device in the top center," he said, pointing. A device like a hexagonal cabinet, measuring three meters by two meters, was emitting a faint light.

Karan came closer and looked at it. "Is it some kind of power unit? It looks like an energy container…like a battery?"

"Then are those tubes the energy source?

"You mean the aliens are the source of the power?"

Desmond said, "They aren't aliens."

Karan and Jena turned their heads. Desmond wore a worried, almost disgusted, expression.

"Desmond, you look bad."

Desmond sighed. His shoulders twitched.

"What is it?" said Jena.

As Desmond lifted his head, the disgust on his face shifted to anger.

"These are humans."

Yuri activated her handy tool when Karan's communication arrived.

"Yuri, come this way. There's something you need to see."

"Did you find something?"

"That's right. I'll send you the coordinates."

Yuri received the coordinates and read them aloud.

"That's where I was going to guide you," said Yukyung. "Follow me."

"What's there?"

"You'd better see for yourself."

Yuri and Kamura followed Yukyung for another ten minutes. The path was flat, and soon the laboratory appeared through the wide corridor.

Karan motioned toward Yuri. "Come here. Come this way." He glanced at Kamura. "Squadron Commander, you'd better be prepared."

"What do you mean?" said Kamura.

"Desmond, show them."

Desmond looked around them without saying a word and activated the panel.

The room grew brighter and brighter. The panel showed the laboratory's journal and log records.

Yuri and Kamura moved closer and started checking the records. As Yuri's expression darkened, Kamura let out a moan.

He turned his head to look at Desmond. "What the hell is this?"

"Is it all true?" asked Yuri in a trembling voice.

"It's true," said Desmond.

"How can we believe this? It sounds insane," Kamura exclaimed.

Karan said with a dry expression, "You have to believe it. As you can see, these people came from planet Han." He paused for a moment, then finished, "They are the victims who were 'collected' during the Big Crush."

II.

"Here's the log of Director Alice Heckerman, the man who ran this facility."

"Desmond, send it to my handy tool for everyone to see," said Karan.

"Okay."

Karan manipulated his handy tool. It projected the journal into the air. A bald face appeared, with dimpled eyelids. It could only be Alice Heckerman.

Desmond read the journal entry aloud as everyone else read along and listened.

"2897 years of endurance, 354 years of the star system. The Diutin fleet that appeared in the third planetary system, Haemosu, launched indiscriminate orbital bombardment toward Han. Due to the overwhelming alien attack, the central government of Han essentially collapsed. Han's air defense system worked, and the space force intercepted it, but to no avail. Not only that, but it was impossible to stop the aliens with the power and technology of mankind. It was more like

a massacre than a battle. It was the biggest bout of incomprehensible violence that mankind encountered since migrating to their new home. People melted, buildings collapsed, and vegetation evaporated. Countless people and facilities were destroyed, along with nature itself."

Kamura closed his eyes. He saw his burning home again. He looked at his hands. He saw himself covered in the blood of his comrades.

"The road to hell had unfolded. The dead bodies formed a mountain, and the smell of burning flesh permeated the air. People who'd lost their parents, lovers, friends, and acquaintances were everywhere, and none of them were in good condition. At this time when it was hard to imagine that another tragedy would unfold, the ground forces of aliens were sent to Han. They slaughtered villagers and soldiers with invisible swords, like lions. I saw the scene firsthand. I can only say it was a miracle that I survived. Yet, the sights I saw that day still appear before my eyes at night and torment me, and sometimes I wonder if this is really a miracle.

"And then the harvesters appeared."

"The harvesters? What does he mean?" said Kamura. No one knew the answer.

Desmond continued reading aloud: *"They were somehow different from the seemingly refined and orderly Diutin warriors who'd attacked Han before. It felt a little more violent and degenerate. Appearing as a harbinger of destruction, they began to harvest the residents of Han, who had lost the strength to resist. Thousands of people were abducted by aliens without any resistance. It is difficult to know the exact number, but it is certain that the unit was at least well over one million. I learned that they were called Harvesters because I met with their members at this lab and heard the explanation. They have been doing this for a long time to harvest the lives of these huge units, and they called it the harvest.*

"In any case, the residents of Han were transferred to this facility. It was only after I had been assigned to this laboratory that I learned that the subjects I met were the inhabitants of the planet Han, the victims of that day. The codename of the project was E-19, where E stands for Egibrios, and 19 stands for the 19th harvest. The word 'egibrios' is a term the harvesters used to call themselves, and I found out while studying their language that it meant 'chosen ones.' In addition, in the Diutin society, they are called 'Propanus,' which means 'the ungodly.'"

"Wait! Hold on a second."

Kamura took a deep breath. Everyone who stood gathered there looked at him. His face was red.

"Kamura, what is it?" said Yuri.

Kamura raised his hand to stop Yuri. "So, you mean that those who attacked Han tried to use the villagers as test subjects?"

"You were there that day too, Land Battle Commander. Didn't you see it?"

"I waged an all-out war with their ground forces. I knew they had kidnapped my compatriots, but I didn't know that they were for some kind of experimentation. What kind of experiment is it?"

"I think we need to look at this log further," said Desmond. "The next log has just been deciphered and we haven't seen it yet."

He cleared his throat and continued to read: *"The absolute majority of those who were transferred were residents of Han, but there were also those of different origins. Most of them were reactionaries, political prisoners and separatists, and some subjects had developed superpowers after making contact with the extraterrestrials. Those who showed remarkable self-discipline and ability were again called up to the Allies and had the opportunity to be trained, but usually not. In general, the minds of the telekinetic powers were extremely unstable, and the personnel trying to control them suffered damage. They were thoroughly treated as subjects and prisoners, and they were imprisoned and gradually died."*

"The vast majority of telekinetic powers must have been the victims of Han who faced the Diutin warriors in person," Jena muttered in a bitter tone.

Yuri thought of Danny.

Danny had always said he remembered the evening of the day he killed Depressed Joe. After killing Joe, Danny also became extremely mentally unstable, and ironically, the Alliance's hero suffered from anxiety. She felt a bit of guilt at the fact that she had deceived him, and that she had left him behind. *Danny, I hope you don't get caught up in the middle of this journey when you don't know what the ending might be.*

In the next moment, Yuri completely forgot about Danny.

"Among the prisoners sent by the Union government to this facility was Kiliman Ivanov, the man who was the President's greatest enemy."

"Yuri."

Karan touched her shoulder and called her again.

"Yuri."

Yuri raised her head and looked around at her squadron and the Brotherhood. Most of them knew how Yuri was feeling.

Kiliman Ivanov, the man who used to be a great politician of the Union, had disappeared shortly after the Big Crush. The man Amon Soros feared most.

Yuri and Irina's father. The man who comforted Yuri when she cried in her hammock at the summer villa.

And the man who disappeared into darkness.

"Amon Soros! That motherfucker killed Kiliman, didn't he?" Kamura cried, clenching his fists in anger.

The men gathered there groaned, lamented, and cursed the Union and Amon Soros.

Desmond glanced at Karan. "Should I continue?"

Karan nodded and squeezed Yuri's shoulder again. "Yuri, I know how you're feeling right now. Even if it's painful and difficult, we should read the rest of this journal. Do you understand what I'm saying?"

Yuri looked at Karan. For a brief moment, unfamiliar emotions flashed across her face. A muffled voice came out of her mouth.

"I…"

Karan nodded as she shut her mouth. "I understand."

Yuri saw the campfire flickering in the villa. She saw and smelled the warm hot pots and dishes her father gave her. She saw herself as a young child held by her father, who had returned with a fishing rod.

She saw the white body of a dying sea creature swallowed up in the dark. The light faded from the creature's body.

Darkness swallowed the light.

Yuri swallowed hard, not knowing exactly what she was saying. "Continue."

Desmond took one breath and continued to read the journal. He was almost halfway through.

"…*we started experimenting. The President is very inter-*

ested in the Deckerman Institute and its projects. When our research topics and content are made public to the world, we will not escape criticism. I too felt a great sorrow for the fate of the subjects. However, this study is necessary for our species to survive in the vast and lonely world of death called the universe. Even if we need human souls to accomplish it.

"This will be a great turning point in human history, and it is the only way we can develop human civilization on a cosmic scale."

"What the hell is this is all about?" said Jena.

Desmond didn't know, so he carried on: *"…Dark energy is a force that is widely spread throughout the universe, but its existence has been difficult to ascertain, and we haven't been able to used it—until now. With the help of the President and the aliens, an uncharted territory lies before us. These specimens are catalysts for the ultimate energy source. A necessity for such a power that is inexhaustible, that can take us anywhere in the universe and change the nature of planets. I was convinced. Especially the Egibrios became convinced when they got involved in this project.*

"Yes. Kiliman Ivanov and the inhabitants of Han are sacrifices for the production of dark energy."

A long silence stretched in the laboratory. No one said a word.

The silence was broken by Junkou's voice coming through Yuri's comm link.

"Captain, this is Junkou. It's urgent."

"Junkou?" said Yuri. "What's going on?"

"Movement and energy not previously sensed are being detected throughout the lab facilities. In addition, a ship just appeared and landed on top of the lab. It appears to be the Allied forces."

"Okay." Yuri's heartbeat picked up as she said to the crew, "I think the Allied forces will be here soon. I will retrieve that journal and read the rest later. We need to move."

"There's a lot more to check…but I think I know what this damn place is," Karan said. "Yuri, what do we do?"

Yuri was thinking about the final contents of Alice Heckerman's journal. *Father.*

She came back to reality.

"Yukyung, how do we get out? Tell me."

Yukyung's complexion was pale. She bit her lip. "It's no use. We're all going to die here."

"I beg your pardon?"

Kamura frowned. "Yukyung, this attitude is not helpful at all. Please cooperate."

"Squadron Commander, don't you feel it?"

"What do you mean?"

"Death is coming." Yukyung shook her head. She could feel Yeonwoo. "Death will come over here! Why doesn't anyone feel it?"

Karan spat out a swear word. "You're acting like a crazy woman!" He gave orders to the Brotherhood. "Secure the exit. Move right away, Yuri."

Yuri sent a message to Junkou. "Re-scan the altered structure here, Junkou. Help us get out of here."

"Okay, Captain."

The lab shook. The oscillations started off weakly and then repeated with increasing intensity. Yuri staggered once, then caught her balance again.

"What's going on?" Jena shouted.

"Everyone, be careful!"

Steel plates and structures partially collapsed from the

ceiling.

"Damn it! Get out of here! Get out!"

The Brotherhood and the land squadron fired bullets toward the exit. As the exit began to close, everyone started running toward it. Meanwhile, Desmond grabbed the log file and stuck it in his handy tool.

As the lab collapsed, some of the crewmembers left behind screamed and disappeared.

Yuri and the others ran out into the wide central aisle. There were several routes. Junkou shouted directions into Yuri's ear.

"Move to the left."

They kept running.

"Wait, stop!" cried Junkou. "The structure is changing again."

A wall began to form in front of their path.

"Junkou, hurry up!"

"Go through the narrow road on the right. It's the only one there. After that, you'll see a staircase leading to the lower level.

"Okay."

As Yukyung ran, she saw ghosts. The ghosts of her deceased companions were calling her. They all beckoned Yukyung to join them. She squeezed her eyes shut for a moment, trying to ignore them.

Infinite darkness will come upon the living.

"There's a staircase!" Karan exclaimed.

"If you go down the stairs, you'll find an elevator right away," said Junkou. "It's the elevator you went down in earlier. Get out of there!"

As they began to move, someone came up from the other side of the stairs. The group stumbled to a stop.

A bald man stopped at the top of the stairs. He looked at the floor for a moment and then raised his head. The dazed man stood still, staring at Yuri and her crew.

"Who are you?" stammered Yuri. When he didn't answer, she asked in a louder voice, "Who are you? Please state your affiliation and name. Are you trying to stop us?"

The man laughed.

Kamura had a bad feeling. He held Death in his hand, and murmured to it, "Give death to your enemies."

Karan pulled out a plasma cutter.

"Wait," said Yuri. "I think it's Director Alice Heckerman."

Kamura also recognized that it was the man from the log. "Are you Alice Heckerman?" he asked.

Alice laughed. "It depends on who you want to see."

Alice's face changed. His face melted like fondue, shifting into that of another person. The group gaped at him in astonishment.

"What the hell?" said Karan in disbelief.

"Oh my God." Yukyung staggered through the crowd and stepped forward. She said in a trembling voice, "How… you…? That face…?"

"Yukyung," said Yuri. "Do you know this man?"

The scar on his left temple; his thick chest and familiar gait. He was the man Yukyung had longed to see.

"Yeonwoo!"

Yeonwoo laughed again.

12.

The man who was Yukyung's lover and a member of the Root Restorationists looked around at everyone with a relaxed expression. When he smiled, Yukyung's heart fluttered.

"Nice to meet you, guests. I came to meet you on behalf of the owner of this facility. Did you like this place?"

"You know the owner?" asked Yukyung in surprise.

Yeonwoo looked at Yukyung and nodded. "Yes. The owner of this place has been watching the guests with interest. He has been watching you since you came in, and he instructed me to meet you."

"Are you some sort of errand runner?" murmured Karan.

When Yeonwoo heard his small voice and nodded, Karan was startled.

"That's right. I'm the messenger prepared for this moment, Karan Shetty."

Karan narrowed his eyes. "How do you know my name?"

"Master knows everything. Maybe he knows you better

than you do."

As Yuri took a cautious step forward, Yeonwoo turned his head to look at her.

"I am Yuri Ivanova, the captain of the *Moscow*."

"Nice to meet you, Yuri Ivanova."

"What should I call you?"

"I have a name too, but I just want you to call me messenger."

"Okay, messenger. Who is the owner of this place? Actually, first—why do you look like Yeonwoo?" She glanced uncomfortably at Yukyung, who looked far too excited to see her lost lover again. "We believed he was dead."

"This figure is one of the intruders who broke in a while ago. I knew they had something to do with you, so I borrowed it for now to make it easier to talk."

Yukyung let out a short scream. Jena tried to grab her shoulders, but she stepped forward and shouted, "You bastards mercilessly slaughtered my comrades. Then they turned them into monsters that neither live nor die, and ate them up. How could you?"

"It's true. You were an intruder and I had to."

"But why! And why are you talking to us now instead of killing us too?"

"Because the master wanted it."

Yukyung was speechless.

Yuri grabbed her arm. "Calm down, Yukyung," she murmured. "I can understand how you feel, seeing your lover again, but this isn't really him. And we need to talk to him. So, please control yourself."

Yukyung opened her mouth, then closed it again, shaking her head.

"Thank you," said Yuri, releasing her arm.

Yuri spoke to the messenger. "Messenger, I have a few questions about your master."

"What do you want to know about the master?"

"I want to know who he is. Please summarize things like his name, his affiliation, and where he is now."

"This is a difficult request. He doesn't have only one name. Those who admire and follow him call him Egibrius. He also names his faithful servants and creatures Egibrius. It is a name that symbolizes their infinite bond with him, but fools who do not understand his will call him and us by the disgusting name of Propanus."

"If he's Propanus, he's a Diutin. Messenger, is your master a Diutin? Is your master the one called Belaos?"

"That's one of my master's old names, yes."

"What is this facility? As we know, this is under the jurisdiction of the Planetary Union government of the Desirée system. So, what are you doing here?"

"First of all, these facilities were not made by you humans. This planet you call Neptunus was actually once one of the Calebs' outlying planets. The Planetary Union government simply built additional structures on top of it to manage the facilities."

"Then, did you corrupt Diutinians form an alliance with the Union government and take over this facility?"

"Something like that."

Yuri's expression hardened. "What is the purpose of this facility? We have seen specimens that appear to be Calebs here, and we have also found specimens of humans."

"This is the place that will be the foundation of all civilizations. It is a place where we research and produce energy that a civilization must possess in order to exist on a cosmic scale. It is the cradle of civilization."

Kamura couldn't stand it any longer, and shouted, "You aliens attacked my hometown with the Union government! Where's your master? Reveal him now."

"It is not yet possible to do that," said the messenger calmly.

"Were the residents of Han also 'materials' for your experiments in this great plan?"

"Yes."

Kamura pulled out his rail gun.

"Kamura!" cried Yuri.

Before anyone could stop him, Kamura fired the muzzle of Death at the messenger. The bullet flying from the rail gun at supersonic speed ripped Yeonwoo's body to pieces and flew through the wall. Yukyung screamed.

"What are you doing, Kamura?" shouted Yuri.

"We don't need to waste our time listening to that bastard," snapped Kamura. "Did you hear what that motherfucker said? He's been using humans to do incomprehensible things!"

"Yeah. And I should've heard more of them, but thanks to you, I didn't hear them, Commander," said Karan in a cold voice. "You're of no use to us in such an emotional state."

Kamura pointed a finger at him. "You better watch your mouth, Karan Shetty. You'll never understand how my people feel."

"You think so? Although not as large as yours, Valhalla made many sacrifices in the war against the Union. I think there may be inhabitants of our planet here, as well."

"Karan is right," said Yuri. "Kamura, calm down. I'm very upset too, but we need to find out more about them.

We need to hear all the stories we don't know."

Kamura looked at Yuri with a depressed expression. "I'm sorry, Captain."

Karan sighed. "Now that you've smashed the messenger, what are we supposed to do now?"

"I don't think you need to worry. Captain," said Jena. "Look over there."

The eyes of those gathered there followed Jena's finger. They saw a terrifying sight.

The fragmented body of Yeonwoo was moving individually. The pieces of his corpse moved like amoeba masses and soon began to clump together. The texture was so distinct that it made Yuri nauseous.

"What the hell is that…?" Desmond murmured.

The pieces that came together soon took on the shape of Yeonwoo again. He stroked his body for a moment, then got up and looked at them.

He had a very calm face, and spoke in a calm voice. "Now it's my turn to ask a question."

Yukyung had fainted. Jena supported her body.

"What question?" asked Yuri.

"It is simple. Are you the ones my master has been waiting for?"

"What?"

"I asked if you were the ones the master has been waiting for."

Yuri and the crew looked at each other in confusion.

"Messenger, if that's your question, we can't answer it," said Yuri.

"Why not?"

"We don't know who your master has been waiting for."

"My master has been waiting for his 'part.'"

A brief expression flashed across the messenger's face for an instant. Yuri recognized it as mourning. It was the first emotion the messenger had shown.

"Part?"

"Yes. Master is looking for the part he lost."

"What is it?"

"It is the power that makes the master the master. It was the original master's power, and it is the power that sustains the universe and can destroy or create all things."

"You mean your master, Belaos, lost it."

"Yes. The master was lost on the planet Black Cygnus twenty years ago in your time, humans. I believe you have another name for it—Han."

Kamura's eyes widened. "Planet Han?"

"Yes, and that power is certainly in this system. A power that has lost its master is about to return to find its master. So, we have been waiting for you. Maybe some of you may have traces of it. I believe I can feel the traces in you, Yuri Ivanova."

"You feel it from me?"

"Yes. Maybe you, or perhaps someone close to you. I'll have to check it out." The messenger stepped forward.

Kamura turned on the plasma cutter. Plasma spurted out and scattered light on the wall. The shadows flickered irregularly.

"Get away, messenger."

The messenger smiled. "It can't kill me, Karan Shetty. Your technology can't even scratch me, my comrades, or my master's servants, let alone kill them."

"Then I'll keep cutting you until I die."

Kamura also aimed his rail gun.

"Please don't," said the messenger. "I'm not trying to

harm you. I'm just trying to connect you with Egibrios's Infinite Intelligence. Then you can see in an instant whether you have the master's shadow."

Yuri shook her head. "I'm sorry, but how do you know what's going to happen? Besides, after the things we've seen in this place…how can we trust that you won't want to use us as 'materials'?"

"You won't be able to leave this place if I don't allow it anyway, Yuri Ivanova." The messenger smiled again. "And you don't have to worry. They're different."

"What?"

Before Yuri could hear an answer, Kamura's railgun flashed again. It ripped the messenger into pieces, and this time, Karan grinned at Kamura.

"Good job, Commander!"

Yukyung fainted, and Jena grabbed her to keep her from falling.

"Yuri, call the pilot," said Karan. "Let's get out of here."

They hurried down the stairs before the messenger came back to life. Just as Junkou had said, they found the elevator at the bottom, at the end of the corridor. The group of about thirty people ran toward the elevator without delay.

"Take it up so we can get back to the ship," said Yuri.

When Jena realized that Yukyung had woken up, he lowered her to the floor. Yukyung sighed.

"Are you okay, Yukyung?" asked Kamura.

"I'm okay."

"We're getting out of this place. Let's move quickly."

"We can't get out of here," murmured Yukyung.

"What?"

"The land commander. And the captain. Karan Shetty. We're going to die here. Belaos won't let us go."

"Yukyung—"

"The elevator is gone!" one of the crew exclaimed.

The elevator doors had opened, but the shaft was completely empty. They had no way to get back to the upper level.

Kamura ground his teeth together in frustration. "Damn it!"

"Junkou, where should we go?" asked Yuri.

Junkou's urgent voice came through her handy tool. "I don't know, Captain! The structure of the lab is constantly changing. It's like it's alive. I can't believe it."

"Damn it, move now!" said Karan.

"Do you know where to go, Karan?" snapped Yuri.

"I don't know what's going to happen if we stay here."

"They're here!"

Jena raised his assault rifle and aimed the light toward the rear. They all turned and saw the creature that looked like Yeonwoo standing there.

Yeonwoo's body was shaking and trembling. Its appearance, which seemed to flow like water, gradually changed, shifting into an alien form. It was a Diutinian.

Yukyung recalled the memory of her losing Yeonwoo. "It was him…" she murmured.

"What? Who do you mean?" asked Yuri.

Yukyung looked at her with a helpless expression. "He's the Diutinian who followed me and Yeonwoo. No, I'll call him Propanus."

A transparent blade erupted from the wrist projector of the Propanus messenger. A profound yet cold voice came from his mouth.

"My business is not over yet."

Karan gripped his plasma cutter, snarling. "Neither is

mine."

Yuri and the crew also aimed their own firearms.

A terrible roaring sound shook the passageway.

As if in response to the roar, beast-like cries erupted from all directions. They seemed to come from the depths of the sea. And at the same time, sounds of unknown origin, footsteps, and dragging sounds echoed through the facility's corridors.

"The monsters are coming," said Yukyung, her voice cracking. "We're all going to die."

She remembered the deep-sea monsters she had seen in her dreams. The snouts. They were always looking for food.

The snouts had found her.

13.

The Propanus messenger ran toward the party, aiming the sword on his wrist.

"Shoot him!" shouted Yuri.

Dozens of different types of muzzles spewed fire.

A bullet was lodged in the messenger's body. The messenger hesitated for a moment, then glided forward and stopped right in front of the group. The messenger sliced the body of one of Yuri's crew in half with the intangible sword.

"Argh! No way! No damage?" yelled Kamura.

The messenger swung his sword again, and in an instant the limbs of another crewmember were separated; he collapsed with a grunt and fell still.

Kamura aimed Death and fired, but the messenger easily avoided it. He had almost animal-like reflexes. He turned on Kamura next. The messenger's sword pointed at the wrist of Kamura's right hand, which was holding the rail gun.

Bang!

An explosion occurred when the messenger's sword and the blade of Karan's plasma cutter collided. The messenger stepped back, looked down at the hole in his arm, and then raised his head.

Karan pointed the cutter. "Let's have a swordfight, alien."

"Your technology is primitive. You still don't know how to harmonize your material and mental powers. Even your venerable sword serves only to buy time."

"I'll be happy if I can buy any time. Come here."

After saying that, Karan ran toward the messenger himself. The messenger's sword and Karan's plasma cutter collided again. Another explosion rang out, and Yuri and the others ducked. Each time the sword and the plasma cutter collided, an explosion occurred. While controlling his sword that was about to fly out of his grasp from the force, Karan spun out of the way to avoid the messenger's weapon.

It felt like his wrist was going to give out. Karan instinctively knew that the messenger was going easy on him. The messenger moved too lightly as he swung his sword. On the other hand, Karan's body was quickly accumulating fatigue. He knew that the alien sword slashing his plasma cutter was no normal sword.

It must be moving with superpowers.

"That's right, Karan. You're smart," said the messenger.

Karan's eyebrows rose in surprise. "Are you reading my thoughts?"

"We've all raised our mental abilities to the limit. If you focus on the other person's feelings and thoughts, you can read them. You, who are just starting out at that stage, may one day understand."

"What are you talking about? I don't have that ability."

"Aren't there humans who have superpowers, too? They'll take you to a new level. You don't realize it yet, but you seem to downplay them."

"That's pretty cool."

Karan and the alien connected their swords again.

Yuri, who was watching from afar, noticed how tired Karan. She said to Jena, "Jena! Karan won't last if this continues!"

Jena raised his gun.

Then the wall to their left collapsed with a roar.

Desmond exclaimed, "Look at that!"

A stench emanated from the hole in the crumbling wall. Forms that moved like jelly appeared. They were fluids made up of human corpses. The shapes emitted a stench made of all kinds of limbs, organs, and bones.

The whole group stared at them in shock.

The corpse jellies moved toward them. The jelly touched the corpses of the fallen crew and absorbed them too.

"What the hell?" said Desmond in a trembling voice.

Among the corpses were moving objects in Allied uniforms. They had dark green eyes full of hostility, and all sorts of rotten odors exuded from their limbs.

His former colleagues.

Desmond narrowed his eyes and shouted as he loaded his gun. "God damn it, shoot them!

The guns spit out fire.

More jelly monsters and corpses came at them through the wall. Some of them coalesced and hardened to form human-like limbs. There were also chunks of human form. They approached with unpleasant movements, like moving corpses. Some of the Brotherhood took up plasma cutters and slashed at the jelly corpses. But as soon as they were cut, they merged with the less fortunate victims. The snouts were lodged in their spinal cords and leaked a thick fluid. The bodies of the dead brothers were stiff. The snouts grew and became huge and swallowed them up.

Screams came from all over the place.

Yukyung was frozen in the middle of the nightmare, unable to do anything. Kamura and the land squadron fired indiscriminately to make the monsters retreat for a moment or two, but that was all they could do. The monsters hunted humans without taking any damage.

Yuri yelled, "Jena, shoot the ceiling! Karan! Back this way!"

Jena looked at Yuri, sweating like rain.

"Quickly!" snapped Yuri.

Jena soon realized her intentions, and switched his assault rifle to grenade mode and fired at the structures on the ceiling. The blown adhesive grenades stuck to the ceiling and then exploded.

Karan fired the automatic pistol on his left waist at the messenger. After the messenger escaped, Karan retreated, and the debris of the structure fell between them.

Karan put his hand on his waist. Blood was flowing profusely. It wasn't a small wound. He frowned.

"Karan, retreat!" shouted Yuri.

Karan flinched when he turned around and saw all the corpses. "What are those?" He made a face like he didn't understand what was happening.

"Karan, hurry up! You have to get out!"

Karan ran backward. Personal firearms blazed at the oncoming monsters. Blood, flesh, and the bodies of the jelly monsters flew and scattered. Karan wielded a plasma cutter and slashed and stabbed.

The screams grew louder.

Jena's breathing was getting harder and harder. Tentacles protruding from the jellies wrapped around some of the crew's limbs and cut them off. Jena suffered a wound to his left arm while avoiding the tentacle. Blood flowed out.

"Retreat!"

The party scrambled toward the elevator in the back. Now, there were only about fifteen people left. Yuri smelled a mixture of blood and sweat. The stench emanating from the monsters was intensifying.

The surviving crewmembers stepped toward the elevator. Desmond shouted at Karan, "Hurry up, Captain!"

Karan gritted his teeth and slashed at more of the monsters.

Yuri noticed that the airflow was getting weird. Hot air was gathering in the center of the passage.

The messenger floated into the air. Then he walked up the air as if there was an invisible staircase. He remained floating in the air for a moment before speaking.

"Stop."

And everyone stopped.

Yuri, Karan, Jena, Kamura, Desmond, Yukyung, and the rest of the crew were frozen in place.

Yuri was astonished. She tried to move her mouth to speak, but no voice came out. *How did he freeze us? Is this also his ability?*

The monsters moved again. Slow but with the clear intention to kill.

One by one, the remaining crew began to fall to the monsters. One member had a hole gorged in his stomach and organs leaked out, and one of the Brotherhood had his throat blown away. Some were lifted whole and swallowed. All Yuri could do was stare, silently struggling but getting nowhere.

Blood continued to seep from Karan's side. For the first time, he felt a deep sense of helplessness. Despair gradually spread from the bleeding wound all over his body. They were all going to die here.

The invisible restraints gripping Yuri's body suddenly released her. She gasped as she found she could move again.

"I should arrest you, but that seems rather complicated," said a voice. A familiar one.

Yuri couldn't believe what she was hearing.

At the end of the hallway, Allied soldiers appeared. He was leading them.

Her lover.

"Danny?" choked Yuri.

"It's been a while, babe." Danny smiled bitterly. "Seems like we both have a lot to talk about."

The first time Danny met Yuri Ivanova was at the banquet hall for commemorating the promotion of Director Cao Chao at the Altra Deng Xiaoping Hotel. She was in a cobalt blue evening dress, and when one of his coworkers introduced her to him, Danny knew that the cobalt blue was filling his head. He struggled to find the words he wanted to say to her.

She smiled and spoke first. "I guess the Connecticut hero is a bit too reticent? You don't like me, do you?"

Connecticut's hero, New Sydney's savior, Slayer's slayer. Danny had never liked those titles. They reminded me of Joe's empty eyes before he died. But for the first time, hearing Yuri call him a hero, Danny was proud of himself. He was willing to accept any title if he could talk to this wonderful woman.

"It's the first time I like that title. I think it's thanks to you."

"Oh, really?" She raised an eyebrow at him. "Why is it because of me?"

"Because the mood of the listener changes depending on the intention of the person who is speaking, and the listener's affection for that person."

"Does that mean you like me?"

He shrugged and smiled. "If that's what you think, I won't deny it."

"You're a very honest person, Captain. Don't you think you're moving a little too fast when we've only just met?"

"Fast or slow, in the end what is going to happen is going to happen."

"What will happen between us?"

"Isn't it okay to take it slow?"

"No, I don't really agree with that." Yuri took his hand. "I want to get to know you quickly."

Danny fell in love with her. He knew that she was naive at times, but she also had deep eyes. She didn't tell the whole story under those deep eyes, yet Danny understood. They were the eyes of those who'd lost their families.

Danny was soon spending more and more time with her near Altra. They would go into a nearby villa on the weekends and didn't know how to get out.

To fall in love is to find another self that will contain and support your imperfect self. Danny didn't understand what that meant until he met Yuri.

The messenger lowered himself to the floor. The monsters didn't move, as if he had commanded them to stop attacking and observe the situation. At that moment, Yuri was convinced that the messenger could control the monsters.

The messenger tilted his head. "Danny Carlos. Are you the one who just broke their bondage?"

"You know me? I don't know you, alien. But yes, my telekinesis disturbed you."

"Why? Sura Handler sent you to arrest these traitors?"

"The chief of staff didn't tell me that unknown aliens, third-class horror monsters, and zombies would welcome me warmly."

"I agree with the President. Capture Yuri Ivanova and kill everyone else."

Danny stared at the messenger for a long moment, then pressed his lips together. "No."

Aiden looked at Danny in shock. "Danny, we have to follow the President's orders," he whispered.

"Aiden, look at what's right before your eyes. They're traitors. But these monsters? I think something's wrong with them. Get rid of them first."

Kirox loaded the grenade launcher.

"Don't be stupid," snapped the messenger. "Follow the orders of the President. I am the President's ally. I don't know what you're thinking, but the things here are known to the President, and he wants them."

"What are these monsters? We saw the others trapped in this facility, too," said Danny. "What does the President want with them?"

"They are the weapon that President Soros wanted, the

project codename E. That's what you're seeing right now."

Danny's eyes widened. "Codename E?"

"Yes. E stands for Egibrios, the first word for our people, and from your point of view, it means a weapon made with alien technology."

"You mean what you created twenty years ago when you made victims of the inhabitants of planet Han? Fuck you, aliens! You're the enemy of mankind!" Danny snarled.

The messenger laughed at him. "If I am the enemy of mankind, are the President and chief of staff also enemies of mankind?"

"Yes."

"I beg your pardon?"

"I said, 'Yes.'"

"Danny!" Aiden shouted. "That's treason—"

"I don't care if it's treason. These monsters and corpses are not right. This whole facility is messed up, and we need to fix it."

The messenger chuckled again. "A bold plan. But will you be able to stop my powers this time?"

The air changed again.

Danny realized that the messenger had once again cast a telekinesis binding motion toward everyone there. It was a powerful force. The suffocating pressure entered his mind, threatening to shatter it.

No.

He narrowed his eyes and pushed back against it. All the frozen people, including Yuri, gasped as he released them from the messenger's hold.

"Stop doing that," Karan spat at the messenger. "You filthy alien."

The messenger ignored him. He wore a look of admiration. "Danny, that's amazing. You showed a lot more control than I expected. Did you do that when you killed Gloomy Joe?"

Danny's eyebrows furrowed. The messenger made a funny expression.

Joe's voice came out of his mouth. "I heard a sound. You know that, right?"

"Stop," said Danny.

"And when I came to my senses, people were all over the place."

"I told you to stop." Danny growled.

"Kill me! I can't stand the smell of blood anymore—I'm going crazy."

"Stop it, you motherfucker!"

A telekinetic storm surrounded Danny. Some of the monsters couldn't stand it, and the corpses flew like puppets, then crumbled into bloody jelly.

The alien transformed into Yeonwoo again. His eyes turned black. He staggered as he walked. "Why, Danny? You've heard the voice too."

The voices said death to Danny. Danny believed the voices would one day either kill him or the people around him. Even when he was left alone in his dormitory. When he was with his mother, Nilla, they spoke to him and messed with his head. Danny refused to follow the voices, but he understood Joe.

What the voices wanted was endless death.

Danny remembered looking into Joe's dying eyes as the light faded from them. *Joe, I hope you are at peace. I sincerely hope so.*

Danny looked at Yuri. "Yuri, get out of here."

"Danny—" she started. "There are so many things I want

to say to you."

Their eyes met across the distance.

"Let's do it next time," he said. "I'm prepared. I won't forgive you easily."

Yuri read many emotions in Danny's eyes. Criticism, affection, concern. They were unbearable.

"What are you going to do on your own?" spat Karan. "Are you going to stop them all by yourself?"

"I don't intend to do that, pirate," said Danny. "I'm not arrogant. But only talented people can stop this guy with telekinesis here. So, you need to get out of here so that my colleagues and I can get out safely."

Aiden grumbled. "I never thought I'd die here."

"I'm sorry, Aiden."

Rifleman Lu Xun clicked his tongue. "Once we get out of here, we'll talk again, Captain."

"Captain," Kamura said to Yuri. "We must go now."

Yuri and the crew started running toward the exit. Danny watched them go and then turned his head. The messenger raised a knife and ran toward him. The clumps of monsters moved again.

Danny concentrated his telekinetic energy into his abdomen.

The messenger stopped.

Then the lumps stopped.

Danny, who had expected a sudden collision, raised an eyebrow in wonder. He noticed that the messenger was making a similar expression to himself.

"What are you doing?" snapped Danny.

"It's strange," murmured the alien.

"I don't know what you're talking about. I think you need to learn how to properly speak to another person."

"It's so strange. Danny. Why do I feel my master in you?"

14.

The final trial had begun.

Joshua saw lawmakers detained on one side. They all looked sad and depressed. Giltarion looked at Victoranus and Dunas alternately with hatred. *It's a very peaceful atmosphere.* Joshua smiled bitterly. He looked for Gartrail, but couldn't find him. Maybe he wouldn't be attending this trial.

A large number of *Robespierre's* crew were also present in the audience, including Redhead Miyabe, Kyungsoo, and Alpha Squadron Leader Mei Yang.

"It's starting soon," said Kyungsoo in a tense voice.

Miyabe nodded. "Is this the final sentence today?"

"Final sentencing. They don't follow a three-trial system like the courts of mankind," said the sergeant.

Miyabe pointed to one side. "Look over there."

A corner of the courtroom was getting rather noisy.

Joshua saw politicians entering with a group of warriors. Joshua asked Dayweo, who was sitting next to him, "Who are they?"

Dayweo glanced at the direction he was pointing and said, "Leader Jonius and his bodyguard warriors."

"You mean the head of the Diutin government?"

"That's right. This trial is getting the attention of our society, Joshua. It's being treated as a serious matter that can even bring members of Congress into custody. The citizens of Adola are now watching this trial in real time, outside the courtroom. You have succeeded. Look at the faces of those who are imprisoned. Some are being accused of being Propanus."

"All I wanted was justice, Dayweo."

"Justice always involves revenge. What you, your partner, and *Robespierre's* crew want is not just a sentence of the accused and the peace that follows. I haven't seen a trial in the courts of your human society, but it won't be much different. Every sentence is a different form of retribution and revenge. Look at the situation now. You have revealed the shame we wanted to hide. And Victoranus, Jonius, and Dunas took advantage of you."

"They used me? I can't agree with that. I used you guys."

"Then you both used each other. Anyway, the Truth Alliance took a hit, as many of them, unintentionally or unwillingly, were Propanus's collaborators, attacking planet Han and committing racial crimes."

"Then why weren't they condemned?" asked Cassie, sounding frustrated.

Dayweo frowned. "This situation is difficult for me as well. But our race has not formally established diplomatic ties with humanity. It is not easy to feel sympathy and guilt for those who live on distant stars where we cannot even communicate with each other."

Cassie was furious. "That's a cowardly excuse!"

"I agree. I'm not trying to make excuses, Cassie Ice. But I'm trying to say that it had to be. Our citizens were shocked too. They thought we had erased all traces of the ungodly from our society, but they've destroyed the government system. Who would have thought they would take control and do things like that? After the air strike on your planet, a civil war started in Adola, and it was quite bloody. The civil war didn't last long, but we knew that the darkness of Belaos had not yet been lifted."

"The Adola system and its colonies have been under tension ever since. Everyone was so busy controlling their fears that we couldn't afford to worry about you. And then, Joshua appeared with scars that had been forgotten and buried. We were cowardly. But you cannot ignore the truth that has been revealed. Because even if someone wants to hide it, it cannot be hidden. Yudians in particular. We actually didn't think about it on purpose; we just ignored it."

"Because of the connected intelligence, right?" said Cassie.

"Yes. That makes it particularly difficult for Adola to forget social events." Dayweo exhaled a deep breath. "Now we begin, Joshua."

"The final trial begins," Dunas called out, right on cue. "We'll start by hearing from the Truth Alliance side."

A young senator Diutin stepped forward. "I am Dame, a member of the Truth Alliance. I will start a defense of the four members, including Giltarion, Dianne, and Caius."

Dunas motioned for him to continue.

"First of all, I will refute the allegations of Propanus against them. The members just mentioned have been accused of being Propanus, and of being collaborators of the Baruar government at the time. However, that is not true. The Alliance of Truth was born when the forces of Velatrias and Zenius waged a civil war with Belaos and his followers. As you know, the truth about the fact that Belaos led the Caleb army and attacked the Yudians is unequivocally clear. The Truth Alliance was the light of the people, and the only hope that the tribe could endure in the turbulent and cold season. Over a thousand years after that, the Truth Alliance was still alive and well, and its members were members of our people. The members of the Truth Alliance were enemies of Belaos."

"The second thing I would like to point out is the question of the intentionality of the results. Humans are still weak in power, and have not formally established diplomatic ties with us. Also, our unfortunate past with them is actually close to an accident. Now, if we condemn or impeach all those involved at the time, as said by the people who came here and the defendant Hypkeranos, who was the Vice Captain of the Adola Defense Force, it is sure to have a significant impact on our society, in a bad way. Sometimes the truth must be condoned for the sake of efficiency and for the sake of the group. And especially if it is the result of an accident. Instead, we will learn to be more careful after this event."

"The universe is infinite and there are always opportunities and dangers at the same time. Although our people have developed civilization for many years, we have only encountered two kinds of intelligent life. Now it is the Caleb tribe and mankind that have been left in history. It is difficult to imagine that encounters with different races will always end in a positive direction. If our society's executives were brought to court every time they encoun-tered a different race, who would want to take the lead?"

"The Mother of Civilization certainly wants us to make wise choices. I think the judges will make that choice too. That is all."

As he listened to Dame's remarks, a surge of resentment rose in Joshua. He whispered to Cassie, "Sophistry. If that's the case, if the Diutin people decide to keep the galaxy under their feet, they won't care if they annihilate any race they encounter."

Before Cassie could respond, Dunas said, "Defendant, please make your last statement."

Hypkeranos stood up from the defendant's seat and looked around the auditorium, at the plaintiff's seat and the parliamentarian's seat. His eyes turned to Joshua and Cassie one last time.

Joshua was far away, but he read something in Hyp's eyes.

Hypkeranos was not looking at Joshua. He was looking at the cities and the slain inhabitants of the planet Han that had collapsed in the bombardment.

"Dear Judge, and members of the House of Represen-tatives and audience, ten years ago, I committed a crime," began Hypkeranos.

The courtroom was buzzing. It was an unexpected rush even from the plaintiff's lawmakers and the audience.

Cassie murmured in a bewildered voice, "Joshua, what is he doing? Admitting he's guilty?"

"Wait. Let's wait, Cass."

Go on, friend. I'm ready to listen. Joshua leaned forward.

Hypkeranos raised his head and looked around the circular court, showing his hands. "My crime is not the unauthorized leakage of the assets and technology of my people. My crime is to destroy countless lives and failed to resist unjust orders."

Hyp's tone was calm. But Joshua could sense the turbulent emotions he was actually feeling. They were deep-rooted emotions that had been refined and permeated over many years.

"Some will say that I am innocent. They'll just say I followed orders. It's not that I didn't think about saying that either. It's a shield that's easy to hide behind. The state ordered it. It was the Adola government's order, and we attacked the human's motherland in advance to repel the heterogeneous race that had attacked Adola and to prevent retaliation.

"But our actions were clearly overreacting. In addition, it was revealed that there was a problem with the legitimacy of the power of the Adola administration, which had to present a vision for our people as well as the lives and property of eighty billion Yudians.

"I regret it. I regret that I did not more aggressively resist unjust orders. When the darkness of the times comes, if we accept the logic of the Truth Alliance, there will be no development for our people. Mistakes are bound to be repeated. If we continue to indulge in complacency and passiveness, eventually, even the Mother of Civilization that embraced us Yudians will not be able to lead us back to the light when we take the wrong path.

"Respected Moderator, now we are at an important crossroads. Indeed, the Adola administration was also the elected power at the time. You must formally apologize for their actions and establish formal relations with the humans of the Desirée system. In doing so, we must show the generations to come, not just within our own race, that we are responsible members of our galaxy. We must not recreate our history with the Calebs.

"I take this opportunity to declare that I apologize to mankind for my sins, and I hope that the future of our generation will be one fulled with development and prosperity."

Silence enveloped the courtroom. No one opened their mouth. In the stillness, Joshua felt something hot rise in his chest, unbearably high.

Amy.

He silently called out the name of his long-lost daughter. Joshua never saw his daughter again after that day on Han. He saw his wife Jiyeon dying in the collapsed buildings. Even that was lucky. Most of the survivors couldn't find the people they'd lost. A broken steel frame pierced her neck, which had been caught between the concrete cracks.

As she was dying, she opened her eyes and looked at him with a sad expression on her face. She made sentences with her mouth, but her throat had lost the ability to make sound beyond a hissing.

"Sorry."

What was it that she was sorry for? It wasn't her fault she'd been killed.

Joshua clenched his fists in his lap, and tears filled his eyes. He missed his wife and daughter so much. They were gone, but they'd settled deeply in his heart, even more painfully than if they had been alive for the last twenty years. Cassie wrapped her arms around his shoulders.

A dull sound echoed in the courtroom. It was the sound of Dunas banging his gavel.

"I will begin the judgment of the double trial Nos. 148-12 and 148-13.

"No. 148-12: Report on the removal of assets for heterogeneous peoples. Defendant Hypkeranos, Plaintiff Truth Alliance. No. 148-13: Defendant Truth Alliance for War Crimes on a Cosmic Scale. Plaintiffs Joshua Kwon and *Robespierre's* crew.

"This court decides as follows: Judging from the objective criteria and circumstances, and the actions of the members of the case, the trial No. 148-12 resulted in a clear transfer of assets, and it is clear that it could act as a disaster for the future of our people. In particular, there is no disagreement that warp-drive technology is a key technology that supports the civilization of our people. It is not known what kind of influence other races will have in the future by acquiring it, but it is considered that even if it is, there is a very high possibility that it will backfire and appear as a serious challenge to our race. There is room for various interpretations in various situations and intentions, but the defendant's act was an act of betrayal against the Yudians, so it is appropriate to treat it as a felony."

Hypkeranos's expression darkened. Victoranus had no emotions on his face. Dame and the detained lawmakers of the Truth Alliance, on the other hand, grew more and more excited.

Dunas continued speaking. "This trial is a double trial, and it leads directly to the judgment of No. 148-13. Like No. 148-12, the war crimes No. 148-13, when judged only by objective criteria and circumstances, it is true that members at the time slaughtered many lives. It is not up to the current court to decide whether or not to overreact, or whether the personal morals of the members take precedence over the situation and the state's orders at the time, but it is a matter for all Adola members to discuss for a longer period of time through connected intelligence. I would like to presume that this is a complex issue that needs to be addressed.

"However, the court finds that there were many problems with the legitimacy of the Adola government at the time the massacre was ordered. It is judged that the successor government should be held responsible for the wrongdoing of the wrong government. Otherwise, no one will be held responsible. In addition, many people here were also directly or indirectly important decision makers of the government at the time, so they cannot be freed from responsibility.

"This court decides as follows: The defendant Hypkeranos of No. 148-12 is guilty. The Alliance of Truth under No. 148-13 and the Adola administration are also guilty. Defendant No. 148-12 has a grace period before the sentence is applied, and Defendant No. 148-13 also has a grace period. Defendant Adola's administration and members of No. 148-13 will contact and formally establish diplomatic ties with the human race of Desirée within three months from now. In addition, ten years ago, in the time of our race, the crime of the incident that occurred twenty years ago to mankind is clearly stated, and compensation is required. Defendant Hypkeranos orders meaningful work on the case.

"This court proposes a resolution of the council that each additional trial will be conducted separately for the lawmakers who were co-conspirators at the time, who are currently detained. Court dismissed." Dunas banged the gavel again.

Dayweo placed a hand on Joshua's shoulder. "Congratulations, human."

As Joshua looked up at him, Dayweo laughed.

"I just wanted to tell you. I think it's really good."

"Thank you, Dayweo. But what do you mean? I still don't understand what exactly what happened."

"I never thought that this would be possible. We are an arrogant race. It is very rare for us to admit our sins and mistakes, Joshua. Dunas spoke of the sins of our people. I personally think it is a big event to have the genocide on planet Han elevated to the agenda for our people to discuss."

"Then what will happen now? Will you form a fact-finding team?"

"Indeed. Reparations will proceed."

"Compensation? To whom?"

"Your system government and its inhabitants."

Joshua frowned. "Surely, not the Union government. They're also subject to condemnation."

"It's complicated, I know. Anyway, that will be discussed later."

Joshua closed his eyes. Cassie hugged him. "We won, Joshua. We won."

Holding his second wife's hand, Joshua pictured scenes from the past. It had been twenty years since the light of death came down from the sky, and Joshua was afraid.

Cassie thought of Yeonsu Carlos. Her ex-husband who'd pointed a gun at her with an expression of disbelief.

Twenty years. The years had led Cassie and Joshua to an alien courtroom no one had ever seen before.

"Thank you to all the lawmakers here, the judges, the leaders, and the people," said Victoranus loudly.

Joshua opened his eyes. Victoranus moved in front of the podium and rushed toward the audience. Many of the members of the Truth Alliance had a scolding expression on their faces. Victoranus seemed to think he was responsible for making this happen. He raised his arms in the air.

"Most of the lawmakers gathered here came from faraway federations, frontiers, and colonies for the future of our race, despite their busy schedules. It was a unity that we have rarely seen in recent years. But now, I can see that the future of our Yudians is bright."

Joshua could see Dunas frowning.

"I'll tell you one more thing. The whereabouts of Propanus and the remnants who attacked Durance have been identified."

"Where are they, Victoranus?" asked Leader Jonius.

Victoranus grinned. Jonius tilted his head.

An awkward moment of silence took over the courtroom. A strange feeling spread through Joshua's limbs. An intuition. He got up from his seat.

Victoranus opened his mouth. "It's here."

The courtroom was silent.

"It was me who attacked Durance."

A scream erupted from one side of the courtroom, on the circular structure in which lawmakers were detained. Dianne cut down the other members. He slaughtered all the other senators in prison with him.

The space was distorted near his wrist.

"Isn't that the sword you use?" Joshua asked Dayweo.

Dayweo recognized it too. A sword that distorted space by amplifying the telekinetic power of Diutin warriors. But it looked a little different than Dayweo's. It made a continuous hissing, explosive sound all around Dianne.

It was quite annoying.

"It's in a more sinister form, Joshua. That's different from the intangible swords of our warriors. It's a Propanus dark sword. It uses a telekinesis that burns life into dark energy. It's so evil that after the Great War with Proditor, it has been banned by society. These are technologies no one knows how to use. Look at them."

Joshua looked at the fallen legislators Dayweo was pointing to. Their bodies were already rotting on the floor.

"Their swords are absorbing their vitality!"

Diutinians all over the courtroom took off their clothes, revealing dark purple robes underneath.

Joshua clenched his fists until they turned white. He'd seen those outfits before—on Han, the day of the Big Crush. The eaters who slaughtered villagers and collected their bodies wore those same purple robes.

A dark sword rose from the wrist projectors of the aliens in purple robes.

"Propanus traitors!" shouted Dayweo.

Victoranus flew through the air to join the other warriors of Propanus.

Dayweo exclaimed in a trembling voice, "Victoranus, how could you betray us? I believed in you!"

Victoranus looked at Dayweo with a cold face. "And you betrayed my master, Dayweo."

"Victoranus!" Aureus grabbed his own intangible sword and ran toward him.

Propanus warriors surrounded Aureus. A black light flashed. Aureus fought off several sword attacks, but was struck from behind and fell.

Jonius and his bodyguards moved.

Victoranus rose into the air and descended in front of

Jonius.

"Jonius."

"Victoranus." Jonius wore a disappointed expression. "I thought I drove all of you out."

"We don't die. Neither does our king. My master will see the harlots of your wretched civilization crumble—and the universe, as it approaches its end."

"Where is Proditor now?"

"That's not his name. Don't insult my master with a blasphemous name, Jonius," spat Victoranus.

"He has long since lost his glorified original name," said Jonius. "Do you think all of our kind will recognize you for this? You will face strong resistance, just like you did ten years ago."

"His power is much stronger than you think. Even if you don't acknowledge it, it's enough to annihilate your government."

"He can't come back. Proditor can't even jump from a warp drive in the deep space where we trapped him."

"Is that what you think?" Victoranus smiled as he raised his dark sword. "We found some of the power that Belaos lost within the humans of the Desirée system. He will now return with that power."

Jonius's bodyguards rushed at Victoranus. He disappeared, then reappeared from behind the bodyguards and thrust a sword into their bodies.

Propanus warriors appeared all over the courtroom, slaughtering lawmakers and the audience.

Joshua took Cassie's hand. His heart was racing with fear. "We have to get out of here. Dayweo, help us!"

Dayweo looked at Joshua. Confusion was evident on his face. He pointed to Jonius. "I have to save the leader—"

"It's too late! We have to get out of here now!"

Dayweo looked at Jonius once more. Two Propanus warriors turned in Joshua and Cassie's direction and glided toward them.

"Warrior Dayweo!" Joshua exclaimed.

He ducked to avoid the warriors' swords, barely escaping them.

"Joshua!" Cassie screamed.

Dayweo drew his intangible sword and rushed toward the Propanus warriors. He who cut off the first warrior's leg, blocked the second warrior's weight-bearing blow, then drew an additional intangible sword from his right arm and sliced the enemy's neck. Dayweo grabbed Joshua's hand and lifted him up.

"Thank you," breathed Joshua.

"Where are you planning to go, Joshua Kwon?"

"Let's go to the *Robespierre* ship."

"Joshua!"

It was the voice of Hypkeranos. He landed in front of Joshua. Behind him came the crew of the *Robespierre*, including Miyabe and Kyungsu.

"You protected my crew. Thank you, Hyp."

"Get out of here while you still can," said Hypkeranos.

Cassie looked frantically around at the blood splattering and bodies falling in the one-sided slaughter. She and the other humans turned and ran from the courtroom, following Dayweo and Hypkeranos.

15.

The messenger lowered his sword.

He tilted his head for a moment and looked at Danny. The messenger's eyes widened, and then his lips spread into a smile. His laughter echoed through the corridor.

Danny couldn't understand the alien's behavior. He checked behind him to confirmed that Yuri and the others had disappeared, and silently counted to three. Then Danny spoke to the messenger.

"Why are you laughing?"

"I can't do this. How can I do this? I can't get over it.

"Are you going to tell me something I can actually understand?"

"Oh, I'm sorry. It's a wonderful realization, that's all. Who would have known that you have a wild power within you, Danny Carlos? Part of my master is within you."

The messenger chuckled. His cheeriness sent a shiver down Danny's spine.

"Sura Handler certainly knew what was inside of you,"

said the messenger.

As soon as he finished speaking, he ran at Danny.

"Danny!" Aiden shouted.

The squad members fired their personal firearms, and plasma flew through the air.

Danny attacked the messenger. The idea was to make all the liquid in his body boil.

The messenger disappeared.

"He's gone!" Aiden cried.

"Where are you?" Danny growled.

A low voice rang in Danny's ear. "I'm behind you, Danny."

As Danny was about to turn around, he felt the strangest thing—another body merging with his own. The messenger. Danny instinctively realized that they were becoming one. His body stiffened.

All his senses were paralyzed. The messenger had control of his body. A tingling sensation ran through him.

Danny heard the messenger's fading voice.

"It wasn't your parents who gave you that power. Who are you, Danny Carlos? Do you really think you are the master of that power?"

The messenger laughed.

Danny's consciousness faded.

Danny felt the cold wind.

At first, he thought he was floating in the middle of an ocean. It was so cold and bleak. Danny opened his eyes.

Distorted space appeared around him. Stars emitted rays of light. The light seemed to flow and was moving toward the center. At the center was darkness.

Should he call it darkness? Could it be simply called

darkness, what swallowed even light and time?

A black hole.

Danny saw something moving within the black hole. Numerous ships escaped the ball of a huge, crumpled demon.

"Danny Carlos," said a voice.

It called Danny from the chasm of outer space.

"Who are you?"

Before he could finish the question, Danny noticed. It was the black hole that spoke to him.

"Nice to meet you, son."

"Am I your son? I don't remember having a father like you."

"You are my son. All of you are my children."

"All of us?"

"Yes, Danny. The poor boy you killed is also mine. The kid you think about sometimes."

Danny realized who he meant. "Joe Milligan."

The voice was silent for a moment, giving Danny time to savor his enlightenment.

"Who are you?" asked Danny.

"I became the beginning of everything. I am everywhere, contemplating. In the most secret place of the universe, I tried to control the balance between the new planets and the dying stars, life and civilization by measuring the movement of galaxies and stars."

"Are those ships yours?"

"Yes."

"Are you an alien?"

"Yes."

"Is the power within me referring to telekinesis?"

"That's what your small and feeble people call it. But it

cannot be defined in such a narrow sense."

"Is this power mine?"

"You know the answer."

"It was yours."

"Yes."

"Joe's power too."

"And you absorbed his power."

Danny frowned. "That can't be true. After that, my strength became very unstable."

"It is only your fear that has made it uncontrollable, son."

Danny saw Joe's body. The horror that was deep inside his heart always started with that scene.

"I will ask again. Are you the original owner of my power?" he asked.

"Yes."

"If that's true, how did your power come to be within me?"

"My servants met your father on the planet Black Cygnus. He took away the power I had given to my servants."

"Do you mean planet Han?"

"Yes."

"Who am I?"

"You are the key to bringing balance to this universe."

"Balance? What do you mean by that?"

"A universe full of dark energy."

"Is that what you want?"

"It is. Soon, everyone will want it."

"How did I become the key to doing that?"

"The power I lost within you. When I regained that power, everything was completed."

"Where are you?"

"I've been watching this universe in the shadows of eons of time."

"A black hole?"

"Shadows are not of a nature that can be understood by a simple physical definition."

Danny couldn't even imagine how long it must have been. His voice trembled as he spoke again. "I opened it up."

The voice didn't answer.

"Who are you?" asked Danny.

"I am old," said the voice. "That's why I have so many names. But the enemies who have been with me the longest call me this."

The ships that had emerged from the black hole opened wormholes.

"The worshipper of the left hand. Those who were banished into the shadows and finally became the shadows."

Thousands of jet-black ships disappeared one by one, emitting light.

"Others call me Proditor the traitor," said the voice. "Or the Apostle of Shadow, Belaos."

Danny pondered the names over and over again.

"I have one question," he said. "I need to hear the answer."

"Say it."

"Are you the one who caused the Big Crush and massacred the residents of Han?"

The voice answered without hesitation, "Yes."

Danny was lying down. A nursery mobile hung on the

ceiling above him. It was a dark gray walled room. A place where he could feel some familiarity.

A man approached him. Deep inside the rough textured skin, his deep eyebrows were shading, and his short beard was sparsely growing. The man's facial features were familiar. Danny realized that he resembled him. Or maybe this man looked like him.

"Danny."

The man lifted him up. He hugged Danny and bounced him. Danny tried to call the man, but no sound came out. His weak fingers struggled.

"Will there come a day when you will have a drink with me? Our little lion Danny Boy."

The man hugged Danny and hummed a song. His big hand patted and caressed Danny's back.

Danny felt like crying.

"Danny."

Danny returned to the present, older Danny. Sean Carlos called him one more time.

"Danny."

He saw a young sorrow in Sean eyes. Danny reached out to say something, but Sean shook his head. He glanced at Danny once more, then turned and walked away.

"Father."

Sean's figure was gradually immersed in the darkness and disappeared.

The darkness was distorted around the black hole.

"Danny!"

Aiden slapped Danny on the cheek.

Danny shook his head and opened his eyes.

"Aiden?"

His vision was blurry, but it soon became clear.

"What happened?"

"Oh my God, are you out of your mind, Captain? There's a lot of stuff going on these days, right?

The crew looked at Danny with worry in their eyes.

"What happened?" asked Danny, looking around. "Where are the monsters? Where did they all go and where are we?"

Aiden raised his arms. "We don't know either."

"What happened? I remember that alien approached me…"

"That's all we remember, too. One thing is for sure, he showed up behind you and did something. We all don't remember what happened after that. The next thing we knew, we were back here."

They were in front of the boarding gate of the *Kudo.*

Kirox muttered, "I can't understand… Captain, do you remember anything?"

He tilted his head as he watched Danny tremble involuntarily.

"Are you okay, Captain?"

Danny sighed. The men knew nothing, but he remembered it. The fleet that had appeared from the black hole, and the voice that had spoken to him.

"What are you going to do now, Danny?" asked Aiden.

Danny got to his feet, rubbing his head. "Did all the Discarded guys escape?"

"It seems so."

"Then we need to get out too. The mission is a failure."

Lu Xun, who stood on alert, turned around. He looked pale, almost sick. "Are we failures?"

"Are you sure we can go inside the ship? Don't make

corpses for nothing; let's go back and report what happened. Everyone, get on board."

"Okay, Captain."

The crew opened *Kudo's* boarding gate.

Danny looked around the lab before boarding. He felt a chill. Like there were some important things he couldn't remember.

Hehurried aboard the ship.

Admiral Lou heard a sound in the darkness. He sat up and tried to turn on the lights in the room. He pressed the switch, but it didn't work. The darkness remained.

There was a squeaking sound. The admiral turned on the portable plasma light on the tabletop and lifted it high. The appearance of the spacious prison room was dimly lit.

The admiral's eyes gradually adapted to the light. He blinked a few times, and the figure of a man slowly entered his eyes.

"You…" said Lou.

The man laughed.

"Chief of Staff, what are you doing here…?"

The chief of staff didn't say anything. Lou stood up and walked over to him. He lost hold of the portable light, and it fell. He quickly picked it up and held it in front of him.

Sura Handler was nowhere to be seen.

Lou's body trembled. He tried to stay calm.

He heard the sound of something pulling. It was coming from the other side of his prison cell, in the corridor at his back. He turned the light in the direction of the sound.

A human form appeared beyond the cell bars. A man with a broken arm was stumbling and walking toward him.

God, what is that?

A disgusting stench enter Lou's nose. The smell of rotting corpses. He raised the light closer to the figure.

It was Hogan.

Lou's eyes widened in alarm. He couldn't understand the situation. Hogan had been imprisoned in a special straitjacket in a special cell one floor below him. *How did he get in here?*

Hogan fixed the admiral in his sights. He began to recognize that there was an obstacle in front of him. Little by little, malice grew in his beastly yellow eyes. He let out an incomprehensible cry.

The admiral felt a tingling sensation as Hogan lumbered toward him. *Stay calm.* The admiral swallowed hard. The cell bars stood between him and the monster. Hogan couldn't kill him right now.

Click. Fear gripped the admiral's whole body.

The door to his prison cell swung wide open.

The admiral didn't know what to do. Now there was nothing standing between him and Hogan.

Lou tried to find a weapon, but all he had was the portable plasma light. All sorts of thoughts swirled in his head and adrenaline rushed.

The smell got worse.

Hogan ran toward him.

16.

Puree was leaving the orbit of the red giant at full speed with its sub-light engine running. Eventually, the frigate was at the last edge of the planetary system.

"Junkou," said Yuri. "How long until we reach Ganesh?"

"It looks like it will take another day."

"Can't we go any faster?"

"We're at the maximum speed."

"Okay. If you see anything unusual, please report it immediately."

"Will do, Captain."

Yuri left the control room and moved to the crew area. They all looked up at her when she walked through the door.

"How's Karan?" she asked.

Jena sighed. "I don't know, Yuri. There don't seem to be any abnormalities on the outside, but I still have a bad feeling."

Karan was lying on a makeshift bed in the corner of the

cabin. Sweat ran down his face.

"Did you administer the decontamination procedure and antibiotics?" asked Yuri.

"Yes," said Jena. "He's still not recovering. I don't know if the site is infected with some extraneous bacteria we don't know about."

"Damn it," said Desmond. "It must have been that alien thing."

"I think so too. I don't know what, but there must have been something," Jena said, his face pale. "When we get back to Ganesh, we'll have to get him checked out."

"We won't be there for one more day," said Yuri

Jena grimanced. "I don't know if he has that much time."

"Damn it, we need to go as fast as possible," Desmond clenched his fist in frustration.

"Did you send any communication as well?" asked Kamura.

Yuri looked at him. "Communication?"

"The facts we saw on Neptunus, and the weapons and monsters they hid. I don't know what good it will do, but we should send a message to Ganesh telling them to be prepared."

"I sent a message right after takeoff. But again, it will only arrive a few hours before we arrive. Because of the distance."

"It's frustrating. If only the *Robespierre* had been there to help us."

"I know, Kamura."

Kamura shook his head. "The Union won't take things slow now that we know their secrets. They'll launch a fierce offensive against us."

"I'm sure they will. We need to come up with a plan. I

hope Captain Joshua comes quickly."

Karan moaned in the corner. "Yuri…"

"Karan?"

The pirates, Yuri, and Kamura approached him. Karan trembled and opened his eyes and said, "I have something to tell you."

"Just me?" asked Yuri.

"Just you."

Yuri glanced at the pirates. Jena nodded and motioned for the brothers to leave. They left, and Kamura followed them out of the cabin.

Yuri sat beside Karan's bed. "You don't look good, Karan."

"I'm going to die."

"Don't die. I still need you."

"It's such an honor to hear you say that. It almost sounds like, 'I love you.'"

"It's not like that."

Karan frowned. "Yuri," he murmured.

"What is it?"

"I loved you."

Yuri didn't know what to say.

"If you hadn't come to Valhalla, I wouldn't be where I am today," said Karan. "You reminded me of who I am, Yuri. So, when you came back, I was happy inside."

Karan looked at Yuri and saw her as a child. A little girl who longed for a future among the sandstorms. After she left, the future she had always thought of had faded like an old photograph.

"Karan." A piece of Yuri's heart was suffocating. She took his hand.

"I helped you, no, my brothers and I helped you because

they still think of you as a brother. A symbol of resistance, Kiliman Ivanov's daughter, Yurina Ivanova. Your original name."

Yuri smiled self-consciously. "Few people know that I changed my name to a masculine one when I came to Valhalla to become stronger myself. Except for you, only my sister knows. It's funny, isn't it? You have a woman's name, while I've become a woman with a man's name."

Karan put on a bitter expression. He groaned violently all of a sudden.

"Are you okay?" she asked, her stomach clenching.

"It's okay, Yuri. I have a question for you."

"Are you going to ask it?"

"Irina, your sister. Where is she? Governor Sakai is waiting for her."

"I don't know. I've barely been in touch with her for the past a few years. I used to think she was dead."

"Have you not met in person?"

She shook her head. "She said she was being chased by the Union government. I wanted to help her, but she wouldn't tell me where she was."

"Are you sure that the person you contacted is your sister?"

"She knew facts from the past that only me and my sister knew. So, I swore I'd find her once this is all settled."

Karan sighed. "I don't think it's going to be cleared up any time soon. Watching Amon Soros's plans with him and the Allies."

"We'll defeat him, Karan. I promise you we will."

Karan closed his eyes and shook his head. Yuri squeezed his hand tighter. After a while, Karan opened his eyes again and looked at her.

"Where are you hurting, Karan?" she asked.

"Your body is strange. Ever since you left Valhalla."

"I hate death. Especially when the people around me die."

She thought of Dallas, the *Moscow* Alpha Leader.

"Do you think I'm going to die that easily?" Karan chuckled and coughed. "That Allied guy. Danny Carlos?"

"What about him?"

"Are you in love with him, Yuri?"

She didn't answer.

"Do you love me?" asked Karan.

"Do I have to answer, Karan?"

"Ha, it's not fair. I tried so hard to win your heart, but I guess I was a fool. Love is never easy." Karan smiled bitterly.

Yuri sensed that he was hiding what he really wanted to say.

"Karan, what do you want to say? This isn't like you. Just tell me."

"Make sure to keep our promise. That's what I wanted to say."

"The promise about New Sydney?"

"Yes. The planet belongs to the brothers."

"I never actually agreed to that, Karan. It's a perilous ambition to take over that planet."

Karan growled. "You must keep your promises, or I will destroy all your new colleagues."

"I'll think about it, but we're not even halfway to discussing it, you know, Karan?"

"I know. And actually, I have one more thing to ask you."

"Yes? What is it?"

Karan shut his mouth. He thought for a moment and frowned. He rolled his eyes. "I've changed my mind."

"What?"

"I was going to ask you a favor, but…I don't want to die. It's not fair. I'll survive, so don't worry about it. I'm too annoyed to die right now."

"What do you mean?"

"Go away. Leave me to rest."

"Karan?"

"Get out."

Karan turned his head toward the wall.

Yuri looked at him for a moment and then said, "Okay."

She got up and left the cabin.

"Captain?" Junkou called to her over her handy tool. "I think you should come to the control room."

"What's going on?" asked Yuri.

"A number of ships have appeared outside the orbit of the planetary system."

"What? Whose ships?"

"I don't know. One thing is for sure, they don't seem like ships made by humans."

"I'll be right there."

Yuri hurried to the control room.

Junkou concluded with a tense voice, "I have a bad feeling, Captain."

Jinsoo, who was in his Ganesh office, confirmed that an emergency communication had come from the *Canberra* and started the communication equipment.

"Jinsoo? This is Theresia."

"Theresia, are you seeing the same thing I am seeing now?" said Jinsoo.

"I think so. Where did those ships at the edge of the system come from?"

"I have no idea. Do they look like Alliance ships?"

"I don't know, but I don't think so. Those ships just popped up out of nowhere. That means they used warp drives."

Ari, who was sitting next to Jinsoo, breathed in. "Doesn't that mean aliens?"

"Damn it, are they from Diutin?" said Theresia.

"I don't know," said Jinsoo, "but I think we need to prepare. We need to put the entire fleet into a mobile stance."

"But there's no Captain Yuri or Karan Shetty, right?" said Ari.

"We'll have to do what we can with the people we have. We'll let the governor know right away."

"Okay."

"Theresia, I will prepare on the ground. Let's keep in touch."

"Will do."

Communication cut off.

Ari looked at Jinsoo with a puzzled expression. "They must be Diutin, right?"

"There's a good chance that's the case. But lately, those aliens have only appeared once, when the *Robespierre* attacked New Shanghai. And then there was only one. There was only other one time when so many ships appeared like they're doing now."

"The Big Crush," murmured Ari.

Jinsoo nodded. His anxiety grew more and more. He pressed the call button in his seat and designated the governor's room.

But he didn't have to. Just then, someone knocked on his office door. When Jinsoo opened it, Governor Sakai staggered inside and shouted, "Dead!"

"What? Who's dead?"

"Admiral Lou! He was murdered!"

Seeing Jinsoo's shocked expression, Sakai shook his head.

"Are you serious, Governor?" said Ari, jumping up. "Who the hell did that?"

"I'm telling the truth," said Sakai, as if he couldn't believe it himself. "And Lou was killed by someone we know!"

"Who is that?" asked Jinsoo.

"Hogan!"

Jinsoo's body went cold. "What?"

"Someone released Hogan," said Sakai, trembling. "Do you understand what I mean, Jinsoo? Your colleague Hogan came up the floor like a prowling cat and ripped Admiral Lou, the poor man, to pieces!"

Yukyung opened her eyes.

Someone was calling her.

She got up from her seat.

"My daughter."

Yukyung shook her head. This was absurd.

"My daughter."

"Who is it? Why are you calling me?"

It was a snout The snout was calling her again. Yukyung closed her eyes.

"You know me, my poor child."

Yukyung knew. Before reaching Neptunus. It was the voice that had called to her since she was asleep. It was the voice that had guided her in the secret facility of the Union.

It followed her everywhere; she couldn't get away from it.

"You have accepted me, and now I am going to set you free."

It was. That was right.

Yukyung opened her eyes.

"Now, follow where I lead," said the voice.

She left her cabin on the ship and started trudging down the corridor.

"Your shell, you will be freed from the bondage of the material that makes you."

It was right. She would be.

"Go to him," said the voice.

Yukyung reached the place where the voice was leading her. With her dazed eyes, she confirmed where the cabin was in front of her.

It was where Karan Shetty lay.

"Yes, that's right," said the voice. It sounded like it was grinning.

17.

The city of Adola was a mess. The purple robes and Diutin warriors were intertwined in battle. A locomotive equipped with a photon cannon glided down the street and opened its gun gates. Hypkeranos lifted his head at the deafening explosive and saw a group of interceptors flying away.

"Those bastards, Hypkeranos!" Dayweo shouted and pointed to a corner of the sky. Joshua and Cassie's eyes followed his hand as they paused outside the courthouse.

The atmosphere vibrated. A tremor from an unfathomable epicenter struck the building behind them, and slid through the ground beneath their feet.

Large, black, egg-shaped ships appeared in the sky.

"Oh my God," breathed Cassie.

"That's crazy big," said Miyabe.

The closest ship's body was so huge that it obscured most of the sky from view.

"It's a harvest ship…" said Hypkeranos.

"Harvest ship?"

Joshua saw the dismay and despair that appeared on Hypkeranos's face. It was an expression only those who'd witnessed a living nightmare could make. Joshua had seen it before on planet Han, twenty years ago.

"Are those heretics trying to harvest the citizens of Adola?"

Dayweo cried out, "They can't!"

The cover of the nearest egg ship opened on both sides. A long metal body with barrel guns appeared, facing the city of Adola.

The gun barrels of more than a dozen giant ships soon aimed straight at the city.

"They're firing their guns, Captain!" Mei said.

The guns blew fire. Numerous shells from the cannons fell on the city. The screams grew louder.

Joshua realized that the shells were no ordinary shells; they were spores. Some of the helpless citizens of Diutin were rendered immobile by the flying spores. The spores rotated and swallowed up the crushed citizens, stretching their stems over the citizens' bodies. Several stems joined together and began to extend toward the sky. They gradually took on a tree-like appearance.

Adola's warriors rushed toward the tree. The black warriors of Propanus also gathered around it.

At an invisible speed, the swordfighting between the dark swords and the photon intangible swords began.

"Here's a security ship," said Dayweo. "Everyone, get on board!"

Everyone looked over at him. He was aboard a Diutin city guard ship, with his hands on the steering wheel.

"We have to go through the Visitor's Tower like this and get to the Adola Spaceport! Come on. They're coming this way!"

There was no more time to delay. Under the command of Joshua and Cassie, *Robespierre's* crew boarded the patrol boat. Before everyone climbed on, a photon cannon fired from somewhere struck the dock next to the guard ship. The patrol boat spun around. Dayweo struggled to gain control of it.

Joshua spat, cursing. "Damn it!"

He looked down and saw that his crewmembers who had not already boarded were being slaughtered by Propanus.

They couldn't do anything to save them, so Dayweo took off. The aircraft staggered briefly, but soon entered flight mode at full power.

"Oh, Joshua. What is that?" Cassie tapped Joshua on the shoulder.

Joshua looked down from above. Trees stretched out over the corpses of Diutin and Propanus warriors lying on the streets. Branches wrapped around their bodies.

A group of corpses rose from the back of the branch.

"What the hell is happening? The dead are waking up? Am I seeing things right, Cassie?"

"Those are the extorted, Joshua," said Hypkeranos.

"The extorted? What, were they extorted?"

"It means those who have been extorted of their bodies and souls by the Tree of Life. The essence of life they possessed has already gone to the roots of those trees. Those wicked heretics have harvested countless lives in the universe in this way."

Joshua's eyes widened as the realization hit him. "Belaos…is that how he was accumulating life energy?"

"That's right. It's disgusting."

Dayweo, who was controlling the aircraft, said, "How could anyone do such a horrible thing to the heart of their own people, Hypkeranos?"

"Dayweo, I don't understand it either. Victoranus intends to destroy all of Adola?"

Dayweo ground his teeth together in anger. "We were deceived by him. The Durance case and this trial were all part of his plan!"

"What do you mean, Dayweo?"

"Aren't most of the councilors of the Diutin Federation over there right now? The other planets and colonies of the Federation will fall into chaos, because their leaders are gone! Planting the Tree of Life at Durance base was just a distraction. Victoranus intended to infiltrate the court from the beginning, weaken the Mother of Civilization, and then take over the Federation government!"

"I think you're right," said Hypkeranos gravely.

"So, the Diutin government doesn't have the power to repel them now, Dayweo?" asked Joshua.

Hyp closed his eyes for a few moments, then said, "I think you're right, Joshua."

"What do you mean?"

"I don't feel the connected intelligence. Propanus broke into the sanctuary recently, and they must have done something. It means that even the Mother of Civilization can't help us. We can't stop them here."

Hypkeranos finished in a sad voice, "Adola is done."

They arrived at the Visitor's Tower in stealth mode. Propanus had not yet reached the tower. However, the officials of Diutin who used to be stationed there were gone. Only traces of the hastily evacuation from the empty office building and various administrative buildings remained.

Joshua and Cassie met a group of crewmembers gathered outside. As Cassie herded them onto the guard ship, she realized that Yuna wasn't with them.

"Joshua, Yuna hasn't come out yet!"

"Let's go inside and find her, Cassie. Dayweo, prepare for takeoff. We'll join you soon."

"Okay, are you sure, Joshua?"

"I'll go with them," said Hypkeranos. "Get the ship ready to take off as soon as we arrive."

"We can't stay long, so hurry," said Dayweo.

Joshua nodded. He, Cassie, and Hypkeranos ran to the tower's elevator and ascended vertically to the 35th floor. They went straight to Cassie's room and opened the door. But there was no sign of anyone inside.

"She isn't here," said Cassie breathlessly.

They left the room and ran around the floor, calling Yuna's name.

When they reached the south side of the floor, wich faced Adola's home port, Joshua saw a Propanus warrior.

The black warrior was holding a sword and his opponent was Mei, who was holding Yuna's hand.

"Mei!"

Mei glanced at them. The black warrior moved.

Joshua exclaimed, "Be careful!"

Mei pulled out a machine gun and fired at the black warrior.

A bullet exploded in mid-air, narrowly missing the warrior. Hypkeranos roared into the air and landed in front of Mei.

"Take Yuna and get out of here!"

Without delay, Mei lifted Yuna into her arms and ran

toward Joshua and Cassie. The three of them moved back, but they lingered in the corridor, not wanting to leave Hypkeranos behind.

As soon as Hyp pulled out the intangible sword from his waist, the sword of the black warrior flew in.

The slashing began, and a squeaking sound rang out. The two warriors exchanged strikes in complicated steps. It continued like that for several minutes. They faced each other with their swords and fought for strength. Soon, Hyp swung his sword wildly and pushed the black warrior away from him.

The black warrior raised his finger and pointed at Hypkeranos. "Adola is in our control. It's time to give up, Commander."

"Traitors. You may think you've won, but the war has only just resumed. Proditor will once again be cast into the cold abyss of space."

The black warrior screamed as he ran and swung his sword at an unstoppable speed. Hypkeranos could barely see it coming. He was crushed by his opponent's might, and desperately swung his intangible sword. Top attack. Bottom defense. His steps were quick. He twisted his body to avoid another slash, and then swung the sword in an arc toward his enemy's shoulder. A crackling sound emanated from the violent clashing of the sword.

The black warrior stepped back and moved in a semicircle. Hypkeranos did the same.

The black warrior flew at him again, and Hyp jumped to avoid him. As soon as he landed, the black warrior looked back. Hypkarnos gripped his sword with both hands and maneuvered it in a skilled way. The black warrior withdrew one foot back to avoid the attack with all his strength, then returned with a slash at Hyperkanos's hand.

Hyp gave up the thought of defending and threw himself at the Propanus warrior. The enemy's sword struck his shoulder and injureed him. Hyp used his telekinetic power to push the warrior away so he could catch his breath, but the black warrior came right back. Hyp held his sword at a medium height and made a right flank cut. He lost control of the sword, though, and it went flying.

The screams of humans were heard from somewhere nearby.

Hyp crouched, peering at the black warrior. His workmanship left something to be desired. Hyp's wound wasn't deep; the problem was that he no longer had his sword.

The black warrior raised his own sword high, ready to make the final strike.

Hypkeranos wasn't ready to give up. He concentrated all his telekinetic energy and wrapped it around the body of the black warrior. The black warrior resisted, but Hypkeranos was stronger.

As he threw the black warrior out of the tower, shattering the glass, Hypkeranos shouted, "Shoot him, Dayweo!"

A guard ship rose and fired its main gun at the black warrior.

The warrior's body was torn apart. His screams created an echo of youthful cruelty.

Cassie took Yuna from Mei and hugged her. Cassie touched Yuna's face with concern.

"Are you okay, my daughter? No injuries?"

Yuna closed her mouth with a stubborn expression. "I'm fine, Mom."

"I was a little surprised, but Yuna did well," said Mei,

sounding proud. "She didn't cry once."

"Thank you for looking after her, Mei," said Cassie. "Seriously."

"No problem." Mei smiled.

Hypkeranos came over to them and said to them, "We're running out of time. We've got to go straight to the spaceport."

The guard ship approached the side of the broken glass on the 35th floor.

Joshua pointed to it. "Everyone, let's go."

The Adola Spaceport was also taken over by the black warriors.

Dayweo and Hypkeranos took the lead, followed by the rest of the crew. The humans had to be constantly vigilant because most of them had no weapons.

The ship docks were in the form of spiral arms. When they arrived at the dock of *Robespierre*, the black warriors were holding the entrance to the dock. They hung back behind a corner, trying to stay out of sight until they formulated a plan.

"We'll have to deal with them before we can take off."

As Hypkeranos spoke, Dayweo nodded.

"I'm going into battle."

"You against all of them? That's a reckless idea, Dayweo."

"But Commander, we have no way to get out of Adola other than that ship."

Joshua looked around and said incredulously, "Humans without weapons will only get in the way. I'm sorry, Hyp. I can't help."

"I didn't expect you to, Joshua. Dayweo, how many are there?"

"It looks like there are twenty."

"Can you deal with that many?"

Dayweo thought for a moment, then pulled out his intangible sword.

"I'll do it, Commander."

The black warriors gathered at the entrance of the dock started running toward them. It was Redhead Miyabe who noticed them first.

"They've seen us!" cried Miyabe.

Out of nowhere, another group of warriors landed in front of Hypkeranos and Dayweo through telekinetic power. There were more than a dozen of them. Hyp looked in disbelief at the male Diutin who was commanding them.

"Gartrail?"

"Nice to see you again, Commander."

Gartrail smiled once at Hypkeranos and pointed his sword at the black warriors.

"For Selim!"

Selim's warriors ran toward the black warriors with their swords pointed forward. Hyp and Dayweo also came to their senses and ran after them. Selim's warriors were not afraid of the black warriors. Rather, their momentum rose and they quickly subdued the Propanus warriors. Hyp and Dayweo also swung their swords like crazy.

The last black warrior's body was pierced by Gartrail's sword. Blue blood flowed out. Gartrail shook it off his sword and threw the black warrior to the side of the dock. Cassie was covering Yuna's eyes.

When the fight was finished, Hip said to him reluctantly, "Thank you, Gartrail."

"Not a problem, Commander."

"I didn't see you in court. Did you follow us?

"I think I'll have to escape from here too. Can we join you, Commander?" Gartrail pointed to the *Robespierre*. "Of course, I will have to ask for your permission as well as the humans."

Dayweo showed a sign of displeasure. "Sir. I did not know that your warriors had come to Adola. I didn't receive any reports."

"You wouldn't have gotten out of this crisis without their help, Dayweo. I brought my warriors here because I had a feeling they would be needed—and it seems my instincts were correct. Will you let me board, Joshua Kwon?"

The last words were directed to Joshua. He pondered for a moment, but there was only one answer.

"It would be an honor, Senator Gartrail."

"Thank you." Gartrail smiled at Dayweo's distorted face. "Are you coming with us, Dayweo? Or are you going to stay in the mayhem of Adola?"

"I'm coming with you," said Dayweo, but he didn't look too happy about it.

Joshua felt a little emotional as he stood in the command room of the *Robespierre* once again. It felt like a long time had passed. There were a few dead or wounded, but most of the crew were safely on board.

The chief engineer saluted him. "Congratulations on your return, Captain!"

"Nice to see you, Kyungsu. How is the state of the ship?"

"There is nothing wrong with the port main engine and the starboard main engine, and all the main engines are fully operational. The pathfinding module and coordinate calculator for long-distance voyages have been repaired. If you set destination coordinates, we will jump right into the edge of this galaxy."

"Thank you for getting everything back in order."

Joshua closed his eyes for a moment and took a deep breath. Too many people were looking at him.

He opened his eyes and cried, "*Robespierre*, take off! Let's get off this planet."

"Aye, Captain!"

"Main engine upward maneuver!"

Power was transmitted to the heavy body, and vibration ran through the ship. Even though it was an urgent moment, Joshua couldn't help smiling at the familiarity of it all.

Robespierre quickly soared toward Adola's atmosphere. Joshua watched the star map.

Redhead Miyabe reported, "Captain, a number of medium-sized and higher ships are floating in the air above Adola."

"I was expecting that. What type of ships?"

"Pattern red. Unknown. They look like alien ships."

Hypkeranos, who was next to Joshua, nodded. "They belong to the Propanus."

"When you reach a suitable altitude, you need to use the warp drive," said Gartrail.

"But where should we go, Senator?"

Joshua called Redhead. "Miyabe, Adola's wormhole communication is still open. Let's scan the Desirée system."

A tense atmosphere filled the silence. After a while, Miyabe opened his mouth.

"The same pattern is confirmed in the Desirée system, specifcally in the Shennong planetary system. It seems to be Propanus."

"Shit."

"What should we do?" said Cassie. "There's no place for us to run away from them now."

Dayweo spoke up. "Did you say run away, Cassie Ice? Why don't you repel the enemies that invaded Adola and start your counterattack from here?"

Hypkeranos shook his head. "Dayweo, I've heard of and know the dance of the guards, but unless you're trying to commit suicide, don't do it."

"Sir, don't disparage the warrior's honor. If Adola falls, our civilization is effectively over. Even during the time of Proditor, Adola was never captured. Rather, we should risk our lives and fight against our enemies."

At that moment, Gartrail, who had been listening quietly, came forward. "Everyone seems to have a lot of thoughts, but I also have a suggestion."

When everyone looked at him, Gartrail said with a smile, "We should go to Nanat."

Everyone was quiet. Except for Joshua and Cassie, none of the humans knew what that was, and Hypkeranos and Dayweo looked perplexed.

"Nanat? Your hometown, Senator?" Joshua asked.

"Indeed, Joshua Kwon. Nanat is my hometown in the middle of the Bullas cluster, tilted thirty degrees from the center of the galactic quadrant."

"It is the land of heretics!" Dayweo exclaimed.

Hyp didn't say anything, but he felt a little nauseous.

Gartrail continued talking without looking at Dayweo. "If they are heretics, how can I, their leader, be a member of the Federation Council, Dayweo?"

"It's just the result of an inevitable political consensus! You're not like ordinary Yudians!"

"Now then, let me ask the Diutinians and humans gathered here. In this situation, with the majority of the Federation members gathered in Adola and killed or taken hostage by Propanus, who can fight against the enemy? Are there any alternatives to this other than our Selim warriors?"

Hyp raised his hand as Dayweo was about to speak. Gartrail looked at him.

"Sir, you are certainly right."

"Thank you, Adola Defense Force Vice-Captain."

"Dayweo, let's face it. The leaders of all the planets of the Federation are on Adola, and many of them have been misled. We can only trust Senator Gartrail and the warriors of Selim."

Dayweo pressed his lips together. After a while, he spoke softly. "I suppose you're right."

Joshua stepped in. "Then we'll set our destination to Nanat. We'll have to reorganize there and find a way to get out of this trouble somehow, whether it's by war or other means."

Hyp agreed. "That's right, Joshua."

"Miyabe, set the route. Senator, please tell us Nanat's coordinates."

"Gladly."

Miyabe set the route with the coordinates given by Gartrail. As soon as he finished setting everything up, he said, "We need to start the warp drive quickly. Propanus ships are fast approaching us."

Joshua looked at the radar. Sure enough, several dots were moving toward the *Robespierre*.

"Engine charging! Pathfinding module activated! Warp drive implemented!"

Robespierre's wormhole generator created a heavy gravitational force, and a trembling vibration was transmitted.

The leap would take place in three minutes. Joshua noticed the shadows on Cassie's face as she stood next to him.

"Cass, what's wrong?"

Cassie looked at him. "Joshua, that's near the Dark Zone."

"What?" He looked at the entered destination coordinates. Only then did he realize what she was talking about.

"The interstellar death cloud you saved me from," she said. "The abyss of space where Harry Carlos threw me. I can't believe that Diutin's world has been this close to the Desirée system…"

The coordinates they were heading toward were only a few parsecs from the location where the Union commander, Harry Carlos, had dispatched Cassie, under the guise of the Outer Space Exploration Project.

Joshua looked at her for a moment and then grabbed Cassie's hand. "It's okay, Cass. Everyone is together now."

"Yeah, I know. I'm just surprised."

Joshua put his arm around her shoulder and hugged her.

A blue sphere appeared in front of the *Robespierre*, which shook off the approaching enemy ships and began cruising into the sphere. The expanded blue sphere seemed to collapse, then contracted into a dot within a few seconds.

The *Robespierre* went through the wormhole.

18.

Danny and the members of the Third Regiment returned to their base outside of Altra, the capital of New Shanghai.

Noise flooded the atmosphere. Troops from various affiliations were running in every direction. Danny tried to get someone's attention, but no one seemed to care about him or his regiment. As another corporal ran past, Danny grabbed his arm to stop him.

"Corporal, wait!"

"Huh?" The corporal finally looked at him properly. " Are you Captain Danny Carlos?"

"Yes, I am. What's your name?" said Danny.

The corporal saluted him. "I'm Xiaohan."

"Xiaohan, why is the camp so noisy right now?

"Captain, don't you know?"

"My colleagues and I just arrived."

"Uh, a lot of unidentified ships have appeared in this system. They belong to aliens."

"What?" Danny's eyes widened in alarm. "Where are

these ships?"

"They appeared at the edge of the system and are heading this way."

Danny raised his voice. "But what are you all doing? Shouldn't everyone be getting ready for battle?"

"That's why everyone's running around. We've been ordered to depart for Ganesh."

That made no sense. "Why Ganesh?"

"The President issued an emergency order. Those aliens are our allies, and we have been ordered to work with them to attack the rebels of Ganesh."

After dropping his crew off, Danny headed for his A-wing.

"Where are you going, boss?" asked Aiden, running after him.

"To see my grandfather."

"In the middle of this mess? Do you think it's true? Are aliens coming, and the President wants us to fight *with* them?"

"I think it's true, yes." Danny got into the A-wing and started the engine.

Aiden hastily approached him. "Danny, wait!"

"Aiden, I'm naming you the temporary captain. Okay? Go and lead your crew."

Aiden looked into Danny's eyes. "Danny, I'm worried."

"What are you worried about?"

"You know what we saw on Neptunus. Something strange is going on." He shook his head. "If you get a chance, please give my family my regards."

"Can't you tell them yourself?"

"There's no time for that. I think we should go to Ganesh right now."

Danny nodded. "Okay. After I find my grandfather, I'll try to find your family and say hello to them for you. But I can't guarantee anything. I hope we'll see each other again soon."

"As do I, Captain. Thank you."

Aiden saluted him before turning away to board the *Little Boy* with Lu Xun, Kirox, and the rest of the regiment.

After watching them fly away, Danny took off aboard the A-wing. He headed toward the airport where Harry Carlos's flagship was located.

The A-wing made an intermittent beep as it entered auto-flight mode. Danny stared blankly at the numerous A-wings visible through the aircraft window and downtown Altra. So much had happened in the past few days, and he didn't know yet what it all meant.

He decided to call his mother. After a few seconds of beeping, a middle-aged woman's face appeared on the top monitor. Curly brown hair, slightly stubborn raised eyebrows, soft cheeks, and small lips. Nilla looked surprised to see him.

"Danny!"

"Mom. Long time no see. It's me."

"How are you? Why did you take so long to call me? I haven't been able to contact you for a while… But your grandfather just told me that you were off on an important mission."

"Yes, I had a secret mission. I had to go undercover. I turned off external communications for the time being because there was a risk of my identity being revealed."

Nilla frowned. "I don't know why you have to do those kinds of jobs. I've said it before, but I don't like that you act as a spy. No matter what happens this time, I will tell

Grandpa to stop making you do this kind of work."

Danny shook his head. "Mom, you don't change, do you? Anyway, I'm fine and I'll take care of my business, so don't worry too much."

"But where are you? It's been a while since I've seen you in person. I'm going to forget what my son really looks like."

"I'm on my way to see Grandpa. And you're looking at me right now."

"Not this monitor, but your real face, Danny Boy."

Danny furrowed his eyebrows slightly. She was only one person in the world who called him that name.

Maybe someone else used to call him that too, but he didn't exist anymore.

Danny got to the point. "Mom, I have a question for you. That's actually why I called."

Nilla said in a sad voice, "You only call when you need something."

"I'm sorry, but I really need to know. It's about my father."

She was silent for a moment. "What are you curious about?"

Nilla always seemed nervous when talking about Sean. Now Danny had a better idea why.

"About what happened before my father died."

"Why are you suddenly curious about those days?"

"I don't know. Because neither my mother nor my grandfather talks about it. Uncle Yeonsu was the same."

"There's nothing you need to know. That's all."

"Mom. Although I can barely remember when I was a child, I do know that something strange happened. It's no secret that Sean Carlos became…different after being sent to planet Han with his father and returning from the Big Crush."

"Your dad was sick."

Danny's heart ached to see anguish and bitterness flash across Nilla's face. His mother continued to speak.

"Your dad was sick and it wasn't his fault. Your dad shouldn't have been there twenty years ago. I still resent your grandfather for it."

"What do you mean when you say Dad was sick? Was he ill?"

Nilla sighed. "I don't know if you could call it an illness. Your father's disease was incurable, and he eventually died because of it. Other people who were sent to planet Han had many of the same symptoms. Oh, Danny. I don't know why you're asking about this. You know that I really hate these stories, right?"

"I'm sorry, Mom. Actually, I just remembered."

"What? What did you remember?"

Seeing Nilla's bewildered expression, Danny smiled sadly.

"My father tried to kill me, didn't he?"

The memory flashed through his mind, emerging from the darkness where he'd shut it long ago.

"Will there come a day when you will have a drink with me? Our little lion Danny Boy," said Sean. He was only a few years older than Danny was now.

When Sean entered Danny's room that day, he suddenly had a seizure.

"Danny Boy."

Sean, anguished, approached his little baby. He went to the side of the crib and squeezed Danny's neck. Little Lion

Danny Boy cried. The mobile on the ceiling fell and broke.

"Let go of that hand, Sean!" A man rushed into Danny's room. Nilla appeared, screaming, behind him.

The man lifted a heavy-looking pistol and aimed it at Sean.

Crazy Sean stopped squeezing Danny's neck and ran toward the man—Danny's uncle.

Yeonsu Carlos fired the pistol.

Nilla's scream grew louder.

"Danny…" His mother called his name, her voice weeping. Danny felt guilty.

"How did you find out?" she asked. "How did you come to remember that time? You have never remembered that time in your life until now. How the hell did you find out?"

"It's too long and complicated to explain, Mom. And don't get too upset. I'm fine."

Danny comforted Nilla again and again.

"Really, Mom. I just want to know if I remember correctly."

"Oh, Danny. Sean was very sick. He was very sick. Many residents of Han and many soldiers of the Union who visited Han had similar symptoms."

"Yeah. What a tragedy."

"I hope you'll forgive your father. He really loved you, Danny Boy."

Danny pictured Sean humming a song while holding his little one.

Tears welled up in his eyes.

"I know, Mom. Someday, I'll be sure to tell you what I've been through."

"Danny, what the hell is going on? I'm so scared. What's

happening right now? Did you head that the President is broadcasting an emergency? Provisional martial law has been put in place in the city. But there is talk that we may move to a bunker sooner or later. Do you know what's going on?"

"Later, Mom. I'll tell you later."

"Please stay safe, Dan. I can't live if you're in danger."

"I love you, Mom. I'll get back to you soon. If anything happens, go into the bunker with the residents."

He ended the communication. Nilla's face disappeared.

His destination was five minutes away. Danny prepared for landing.

The airport was noisy. Members of various mobile platoons and amphibious assault corps were busy preparing for takeoff, moving and carrying luggage.

The second lieutenant in control confirmed Danny's identity and authorized his A-wing for landing.

"Where is Commander Carlos?" asked Danny as soon as he got off the plane.

"He's preparing for takeoff. He's doing the final inspection in the temporary barracks. I'll take you to him."

Danny went to Harry's barracks, following a private called by the second lieutenant. The temporary barracks were made of sandwich panels and high-strength and lightweight special alloys. A guard standing outside confirmed Danny's identity with his handy tool.

"Come in, Captain."

The automatic door at the entrance to the barracks opened. "Thank you," said Danny, and hurriedly headed inside.

Harry Carlos, who had changed into a neat battle suit,

saw him and said, "You're back."

"Grandfather."

"Sit down."

Harry pointed to a chair at the small side table. As Danny sat down, Harry sat across from him.

"Have you heard what's happening, Danny? Aliens appeared at the edge of the planetary system. I don't know exactly what's going on, but orders were issued directly from the President's office. We're supposed to work with the aliens to eradicate the rebels. I'll be leaving for Ganesh in an hour."

"Like twenty years ago? Are you going to work with the aliens to slaughter humans?"

"I don't want to quarrel with you right now, Danny."

"I didn't come here to argue either."

"How did the operation go? It seems to have failed."

"It did."

"I thought so."

"That's not all. Grandpa, let me ask you one thing. About my father."

Harry frowned. "Right now? Why do you bring him up at a time like this?"

"You have to trust me. It's related to the current situation."

Harry twitched his eyebrows in a puzzled way. "Then tell me quickly."

"I remembered that my father tried to kill me. Please, don't ask me how I remembered. I don't have time to explain."

Danny spoke hastily and raised his hand, and Harry shut his mouth. Danny read the astonishment on his face.

"I found out about it while we were on Neptunus. There

were a lot of things going on there, but in summary, I met an alien. An alien who had a deep connection with the Union. Most of all, he talked about the President's chief of staff, Sura Handler."

"Didn't I say there's extraterrestrial technology out there?" said Harry. "That's not surprising."

"Yeah, but this alien sent my mind somewhere far, far away." Danny trembled without realizing it, thinking of the darkness and the voices he had seen and heard. "I know it might sound crazy, but…he sent me to a black hole."

"A black hole?" Harry's eyes narrowed. "What the hell does that mean?"

"A black hole at the center of our galaxy. There was someone in it." Seeing the absurd expression on Harry's face, Danny hurriedly added: "And the fleets. The alien ships that just appeared in this system—I saw them emerge from the black hole, and then disappear."

"I don't really understand what you're saying, son."

"Someone in the black hole told me. Maybe he was an alien, or a god. Damn, I still don't know what he was, but I'm sure that being sent the fleet here. I know his name. Proditor. Or Belaos. Have you ever heard of it?"

Harry shook his head. "No, I haven't."

"He told me he met my father on planet Han. And my father took some of his power."

"Oh my God." Harry fiddled with his nose. He continued to speak with difficulty, as if he was struggling to keep up with several facts. "After the Big Crush, children with superpowers were born…most of them from the surviving residents of Han. Some also from the Allied soldiers who were dispatched at the time. Many of them became mentally unstable and killed other people or committed suicide. The Union collected and systematically trained those with such telekinesis… Sean did too… You're telling me you think humans absorbed alien powers?"

"That's right. My father absorbed the power of some great being called Belaos."

"I knew Sean had that ability too, and it made him mentally unstable, Danny. Sometimes you did too, and so did that Joe Milligan you killed."

Danny nodded. "This power is definitely too unstable to be controlled by a human body. It was too much for my father. That's why he tried to kill me. And…" Danny ended his speech bitterly. "He was shot and killed by Uncle Yeonsu."

He lowered his head, his hands trembling. He felt an indescribable feeling as he pondered the burden of his life and the source of the power that sometimes protected him.

When Danny looked up, he saw something strange. Harry was looking at Danny with the eyes of a little child whose secret had been discovered.

"What is it, Grandpa?"

"Danny, you're wrong."

"What?"

"It wasn't Yeonsu who killed Sean."

Danny tensed. "Excuse me? In the scene I saw, it was definitely Uncle Yeonsu."

Harry sighed. The room seemed to warp around Danny, and the sound of his heart pounding echoed in his ears.

"It was you, Danny Boy, who killed Sean Carlos."

19.

"I beg your pardon?" said Danny.

Harry didn't say anything.

"I killed my father... Is that what you're saying?"

Harry nodded, his eyes mournful. "Yes. Yeonsu's bullets didn't threaten Sean at all. As I said, Sean had an ability, and it was that ability that stopped the bullets. But Sean, had gone mad, and he was unaware of the telekinetic power of the two-year-old infant behind him."

"Oh my God."

Danny's mouth went dry. He didn't speak for a long time.

"That's a lie."

Harry said in a low voice, "It's true, Danny. Neither I nor your mother blame you. It was an accident. And if you had left Sean alive, he would have killed your mother and Yeonsu would."

"A lie... That's a lie..." Danny shook his head and covered his face with both hands. "It's a lie, Grandpa."

Danny thought of Nilla. A woman who sometimes looked at her son with a wounded expression, ever since he was a child. There was always a feeling of irreversible loss around Nilla and Danny.

It was because of Danny Boy. Because he'd killed his own father.

Harry put a hand on his shoulder. "Danny, keep your chin up. I understand how you feel, but now is not the time to fall into despair. Look at me."

Danny lifted his tearful face to look at his grandfather. A veteran soldier and politician.

Harry Carlos, a poor man who had suffered loss all his life.

"Do you want to talk about anything else?" he asked. "It seemed like you had more to say."

"I'm…"

"Danny."

Danny sighed and gently wiped his eyes with both arms. He spoke in a slightly shaky voice.

"The voice said it was him who caused the Big Crush."

"What?"

"Aliens' technology. Grandpa. They have some sort of technology that uses dark energy. I still don't understand it well, but I think Belaos used a method to collect the energy of living things and convert it into dark energy. So, it caused the Big Crush. They slaughtered and captured a lot of villagers. Neptunus had a facility, some kind of factory, that made that energy."

"Nonsense."

"Grandfather—"

"That's bullshit!"

Blood rushed into Harry's face. He clenched his fists in

fury.

"The Big Crush was caused by me and the President! For the Union!"

Danny felt like he had been struck in the back of the head. The psychological shock was so great that he almost fell out of his seat. He managed to come to his senses and said, "What did you say now?"

Harry continued to vent his anger, as if Danny was no longer in the room.

"Is that alien bastard even controlling us! Don't be ridiculous! We were trying to take over the warp-drive technology of planet Han, developed by the Mining Guild government. Otherwise, we'd end up being lost by Han. Okay, Danny? So, we caused a chaos on the planet and took advantage of the chaos to seize the *Incheon* ship. And then we dispatched Karl Age to the *Incheon*."

Incheon. The old name of the *__Admiral Cheng Ho__* ship, which was stolen by Karl Ryoma. The first ship equipped with warp-drive technology developed by the Mining Guild Government.

Danny put the pieces together, remembering what Jinsoo had told him before, about how the Union was behind the Big Crush. Danny hadn't wanted to believe it, not really, even if a part of him knew it was the truth.

"That's why Uncle Yeonsu left us," he murmured. "Because he found out that you were the slayer who betrayed planet Han…"

His brain was overwhelmed by the sudden flood of information.

"Because…because he found out that the person he had been living with for decades, thinking he was his father… was a traitor."

Harry glared at him with bloodshot eyes and shouted, "Ha! Danny Boy, can you understand? How could I have thought of doing such a thing? It was a perfect plan. It was a plan that President Soros and I carefully executed with many steps in mind! The Mining Guild knew about Duitin. Ignoring the Planetary Union, they decided to take the FTL leap to Adola first to establish diplomatic ties and take the lead in the Union. That was a big moment in our history. The future Desirée system's history could have been reorganized around planet Han. Should we have left it alone, leaving the descendants of those who were only marginal small countries on Mother Earth to take over as our rulers, Danny? You can't go against a great nation. The owner of Desirée is the Union of Planets and New Shanghai. So, we secretly took control of the *Incheon* and sent an interpreter to Diutin who would speak on behalf of the Union."

Danny shook his head. All kinds of emotions surged within him. "Who was that person? What did he do?"

The truth hit him before Harry gave an answer. There was only one answer.

"He declared war on Adola, so the aliens attacked him."

Harry nodded. "The *Gunsan*, *Los Angeles*, and *Incheon* ships leaped to the planet Adola in the Diutin system. They carefully sent messages of goodwill toward the Adola government through the Diutin interpreter Karl Age, dispatched by the Planetary Union, Amon Soros. Or at least, the others aboard the ships thought they were messages of goodwill. And in response, the Diutinians attacked them."

Danny could piece together the rest. The *Gunsan* and *Los Angeles* ships were shot down, and only the *Incheon* returned to the planet Han. And the Diutin fleet followed and attacked Han.

"Was that fleet really from Diutin?" he asked. "Or were they the servants of Belaos?"

"They took advantage of you, Grandpa," said Danny angrily.

Harry looked at him."What nonsense are you saying now?"

"You were taken advantage of. It was a chess game played on a screenplay that Belaos crafted to obtain dark energy. Maybe the President was also played in that game. I don't know. You thought you were doing the right thing for the country, but that's bullshit. After all, you are just a murderer. A murderer who killed tens of millions of innocent people!"

Madness flashed in Harry's eyes.

"Shut up!" Harry shouted and stood up.

Danny shouted too, jumping to his feet. Anger raged through Danny's heart like a storm. Maybe if Harry hadn't helped the President with this plan, Sean wouldn't have died.

Maybe Nilla and Danny would have lived their lives without feeling loss.

"You used to tell me that when you were young, you lost your great-grandparents in a Name War," he snapped. "You know the pain of losing people you love. How the hell could you do such a thing?"

"I was a patriot! I had to make some sacrifices for this country. President Soros understood!"

"Sacrifice? What did you make a sacrifice for?"

"The country and the people, you idiot! It was for the country and the people."

"A country!" Danny laughed. "Are you saying that you killed tens of millions for your country? The state must exist for the people?"

"You don't know anything. Even so, I had to correct the history. It was justice for a bigger future! I just made up my mind to take on a job no one else wanted to do! Tens of millions of lives may have been lost, but in the end, future generations of the Planetary Union will know my accomplishments! You will appreciate how I was patriotic and prevented the strife that would have arisen from planet Han."

Danny couldn't take it any longer. A telekinetic frenzy erupted from his hands and struck Harry Carlos. Harry's body flew backward and crashed into the barracks wall.

It happened in an instant.

Harry moaned. Danny stood there, not knowing what to do with the anger that controlled his body. Then he came to his senses and approached his fallen grandfather.

"Grandpa, are you okay?"

Harry let out another moan. It wasn't a serious injury, but he shook his head and said, "Damn it, it really hurts."

"Can you stand up?"

Danny grabbed Harry's hand and supported him. Harry leaned back in his chair and sighed. For a moment, he said nothing. He looked up at the ceiling. A moment ago, the light had been flickering under the influence of telekinetic power.

After a while, Harry opened his mouth. "What would you like me to do?"

Danny didn't answer. Harry lifted his head and saw his grandson standing motionless.

Harry was suddenly frightened.

"Danny Boy, what do you want me to do?"

Danny shook his head. Harry saw Danny's shadow stretching across the floor behind him. He spoke toward the shadow.

"Yeah, you are right. I am a slayer. I've committed countless crimes. Yeonsu found out the truth. But Danny, please, won't you find a way to forgive this sinful old man?" He lifted his head and looked at Danny. "Huh? Will you?"

Danny shook his head. "You'll have to ask for my forgiveness later. Now we have to save others before it's too late, Grandpa."

He chewed and swallowed what he was about to say: *If you want to make your sins even a little lighter.*

But it seemed as though Harry cound sense his unspoken words. He hung his head helplessly. "You're right, Danny."

Danny looked into his eyes. "Grandfather?"

"I'm going to go to hell. You're right."

Harry hugged himself and started crying. The emotions came so suddenly that even Harry looked surprised. Things that had tormented him for decades came bubbling to the surface. The mask has been removed.

When Danny saw Harry's face like that, all sorts of emotions surged inside him: hate, contempt, love, concern. It was a whirlwind of uncontrollable feelings.

Wiping away his tears, Harry said, "Yeonsu, your uncle, came to see me before he disappeared."

"I know."

"I wish he would've shot me when he pointed his gun at me. He was really my son. Maybe not by blood, but after Sean died, he was the only son I had left. How did he feel when he found out that his father was responsible for his hometown's devastation? I adopted him as my son because he'd gone through something similar to what I went through."

Harry closed his eyes and took a deep breath. It wasn't just a sigh. It was a sigh containing all his regrets from his sixty years of life.

"As you said, if the President and I killed the residents of Han by using the aliens' tactics, we must stop them. The aliens that have appeared now…maybe they will cause a second Big Crush in Ganesh."

Harry opened his eyes. "You have to stop them, Danny."

"That's treason, Grandpa."

"Damn, then what are you going to do? Is there any other way?"

"I don't know." Danny ran a hand through his hair and sat down again. "I don't know what to do."

"Neither do I, Danny. We're going to be executed for treason."

Danny and Harry were lost in thought. Soon, New Shanghai's fleet would go to Ganesh under Harry's command. Together with a fleet of aliens, they would bomb Ganesh and drive out the rebels.

"The President was not taken advantage of, Danny."

Danny pulled himself from his thoughts and looked at Harry. "What do you mean?"

"The President wasn't taken advantage of. It's hard to believe, but he must have known everything. He'd be a staunch ally of the aliens."

Danny narrowed his eyes. "If that's true…"

"Yes, I have to stop him. That way, I think my sins will be lightened even a little." Harry got up. "Let's go. There's no time to waste."

Danny jumped to his feet and followed Harry.

The door to the barracks opened, and the guard rushed in. "Commander! You must come here now!"

"What's going on? Give me a report."

"An alien fleet is heading to New Shanghai. You should go straight to the command room!"

"What?" Harry glanced at Danny with a puzzled expression. To the guard, he said, "Take me there right now."

The guard gave a salute.

Harry and Danny started following the guard.

"What the hell is this, Grandpa?"

"I don't know. Private, what happened?"

"I don't know," said the guard. "An emergency message arrived not long ago. Their destination seems to be New Shanghai, not Ganesh."

"Damn, Danny. We need to evacuate the villagers."

Danny nodded. "I know."

"But where are we going?"

Harry suddenly frowned and stopped walking. Danny stopped too.

The guard was taking them in the opposite direction of the command room. It was the road to the outskirts of the base. No one else was around.

"Where are you taking us, Private?"

The guard turned to Harry. "I'm sorry, Commander. I must have lost my mind."

Without warning, he ran to the commander. Harry didn't have time to react.

A sword protruding from the guard's arm pierced Harry's stomach.

"Grandfather!" Danny shouted.

He whipped out a gun from his waist. The sword fell from Harry's stomach, and Harry collapsed to the ground. Danny fired three shots in succession at the guard.

The bullet stopped in mid-air.

They floated for a few seconds, then fell.

The guard grinned at Danny. "Long time no see, Captain Carlos."

The guard's face became distorted and transformed into a different person.

Danny's eyebrows rose in shock. "Chief of Staff?"

Sura Handler raised his sword and pointed at Danny.

"The President says hello to you."

20.

Danny glanced at Harry, collapsed on the ground, then turned his furious gaze to Sura Handler.

Danny raised one hand and spread the palm toward Sura Handler. "You aren't human."

"No, I'm a human too," said the chief of staff with a slight smile. "Like you. I've only encountered 'the world behind the curtain.'"

"What?"

"Didn't the master show you a glimpse of it too?"

A chill ran down Harry's spine as he thought of the black hole. "What is your identity? Are you a servant of Belaos?"

The chief of staff lowered his arm. The sword disappeared. "Was your meeting with my master not pleasant? Anyway, it doesn't matter. Personally, I am really grateful to you. Thanks to you, my master has regained the power to escape from exile. Of course, that power was his from the very beginning."

"Did you know that when you met me?"

"I did."

"That's why you sent me to the messenger."

"I don't want to fight you," said Handler calmly. "You don't even know the size of your power yet, and you don't know how to control it. You are important, Danny. Come and serve the master with me and the others who follow him."

"I don't want to. You guys are crazy."

"It may seem that way, depending on your point of view. But the master will give you more than you think. Don't you know, Danny? He is omnipotent. Anything is possible. It's your power, Danny; it's really up to you. He can even give you immortality if you desire it."

Danny doubted his ears. "Did you say immortality?"

"Danny, your master was imprisoned in a black hole at the center of this galaxy. The lowly ones who usurped and betrayed his rightful authority expelled him there 1,300 years ago in Duitin time, 2,600 years in your time. That's the truth. How long do you think my master was there? 2,600 years?"

Danny didn't answer. He thought of the black hole and the voice. Sweat trickled down his back.

"In a black hole, time loses meaning," Handler continued. "The master spent a fleeting time there, yet he witnessed hundreds of millions of years—maybe even billions. He is the birthplace of galaxies in which pulsars and quasars quake. I saw the moment. I saw the beginning of the universe."

"It's an incredible story."

If that was true, Belaos would have been there for an unimaginably long time. Both Belaos and his fleet. *How is that possible?* wondered Danny. It was something that couldn't be understood by the laws of physics.

"Now do you understand?" asked Handler. "How about it? Are you willing to join us?"

Out of the corner of his eye, Danny saw Harry twitch on the ground. He was still alive.

Danny opened a telekinetic storm.

"I'll never join you," he said.

Danny's telekinesis wrapped around the chief of staff. He would tear this traitorous man apart.

Sura Handler shook his head. "It doesn't matter."

Danny felt the power draining from his body. He slumped down and looked at the chief of staff, who continued to remain calm.

"What did you do to me?" He gasped.

"I told you, Danny. You don't know how to use your powers properly. Your race, who has just awakened to mental powers, is only in the early stages of using it."

Danny's breath caught in the air. He shook his limbs.

"If you don't cooperate, I'll have to kill you," said Handler.

Danny felt the blood in his body flowing backward. His body temperature was rising fast. It felt like he was losing his mind.

"Ouch! Stop it!"

Saliva dribbled out of his mouth, and a strong pressure built behind his eyeballs, like they were about to pop out.

If keeps doing this, I'll explode and die, thought Danny.

Bang!

The power that controlled Danny's body gave up its hold. Danny fell. When he managed to lift his head, he saw the blood flowing from the chief of staff's body. An arm protruded from Harry's collapsed body.

At the end of his arm was a revolver.

The chief of staff tilted his head toward Harry. "I commend you for your devotion to the Planetary Union for decades, Commander."

The dark sword that rose from Handler's arm pierced Harry's back. Danny screamed.

"No!"

Harry stopped moving.

Sura Handler floated up into the air. He smiled at Danny.

"Goodbye, Danny. I hope you survive."

Danny tried to get to his feet and run at him, firing his gun. Handler dodged the bullet with a leisurely motion and then quickly turned around.

A moment later, the chief of staff was gone.

Danny staggered over to Harry and dropped to his knees beside him, grabbing his shoulders. "Grandfather!"

He turned the commander over. His body was limp.

"Oh my God, Grandpa. Wait a minute. I'll call the medic. No, I'll get you to the hospital right away."

Danny picked up his handy tool, but Harry gently grabbed his hand.

Danny looked down at him. His grandfather trembled and wrinkled his motionless lips desperately.

"Yes?" Danny leaned his ear closer to his mouth.

Harry's breathing was irregular. He had shed too much blood.

In his mind's eye, Harry saw the endless tombs. He saw weeping orphans and wild dogs gnawing their ravenous snouts among the destroyed ashes. It was the image that had dominated his childhood.

He witnessed the road to hell twenty years ago again. Unbearable scenes.

"Danny..." he murmured.

A single tear streamed from his grayish-white eyes.

"Escape...you...idiot..."

And then Harry's eyes rolled back into his head, and death took him.

"Grandfather?" Danny cried.

Harry Carlos didn't move again.

A stubborn and eccentric grandfather with frosty eyes who had killed countless people and spent decades in remorse. The commander of the Star System Defense Force. The right arm of Amon Soros.

Harry Carlos died in the arms of his grandson, looking so lonely.

Danny looked down at Harry's gray face. He couldn't believe he was gone.

The alarm siren sounded. Footsteps, hovers and locomotives began to be heard.

"Danny Carlos, don't move!" someone shouted. "Stand up with your hands on your head!"

Danny didn't know how long he'd been kneeling there on the ground, holding his grandfather. He looked up and saw police officers and security guards approaching him on hoverbikes.

"If you move, we will kill you! Just move your legs and stand up!"

Danny slowly stood up with his hands on his head. He had a hard time recognizing anything that was happening around him.

The military police inspected Harry's body. After a few words, they came up to Danny, flipped his hands over, and put restraints on both wrists.

"Captain Carlos, you are under arrest for the murder of Commander Harry Carlos."

21.

Under Theresia's command, a combined fleet of the Red Wind Brotherhood, the Discarded, and the Root Restorationists prepared for battle over Ganesh. Communication came into the control room of the *Canberra*.

"Theresia, preparations are complete." It was Judy, who was in command of another ship. "Do you have any idea who's controlling those ships?"

"I don't know, Judy. But it looks like they're definitely not our allies."

Just then, a correspondent informed Theresia that a message had arrived. It was Yuri's voice message.

"Theresia, this is Yuri Ivanova. We are returning to Ganesh with all our might on the *Puree*. Some crewmembers have died, but the brothers are still alive. But Karan is unwell, although the cause is unknown."

Theresia paused. He wanted to ask a question, but the message was just a one-way delivery.

"We've got some idea of what's going on on Neptunus,"

continued Yuri. "We know an unidentified fleet has just appeared in the Shennong system. We're guessing it's probably Diutin's fleet. But these Diutinians are different from the ones we know who helped the *Robespierre* escape. They are Diutin renegades called Propanus. The one who leads them is called Belaos, and we have not yet figured out exactly what they want. I'm pretty sure they're 'harvesting' groups of life across the galaxy. They believe they can convert life energy into dark energy, and I think they have. The Big Crush twenty years ago was a continuation of that. We discovered that the inhabitants of planet Han were captured and taken to Neptunus, where they became a source of energy. Amon Soros may have wanted that energy, too, but he is working with the Propanus. And the creatures that are used in this way are reborn like zombies and attack everything around them. We were almost killed by humanoids and monsters of all sorts beyond our understanding.

"Theresia, I hate to imagine, but maybe something similar happened during the Valhalla War ten years ago. It is highly probable that our brothers and families who were taken away and never returned faced this same fate."

Theresia clenched his fists, thinking of the Day of Disaster.

"Theresia, protect Ganesh until we arrive. We must stop our enemies no matter what. Otherwise, I have a feeling that there will be a second Big Crush on Ganesh."

Yuri finished her speech with a tense voice.

"Stay alive, Theresia. And all your brothers and sisters."

The message ended.

All personnel in the control room were listening to the message. A heavy silence descended over everyone.

Theresia opened his mouth. "Judy, did you hear that?"

Judy's voice came through the speaker after a while. "I heard, Theresia. It's so much that I can't even digest it all. But Ivanova, the captain, and the brothers wouldn't lie."

"I agree. The challenge we are facing now is how to deal with the approaching enemies." Theresia sighed. "We can't let the Big Crush happen again. Judy, relay this information to Governor Sakai and Jinsoo Kim on the ground. And send all possible troops into space. And get the people of Ganesh to evacuate to the bunker."

"Okay, Theresia," said Judy.

"Junkou, how long do we have left?" asked Yuri.

"We'll arrive in Ganesh in about four hours."

"Any update on the *Moscow*?"

"The ship is being prepared. I received a message saying that it's temporarily under the command of Haneul Bravo."

"And what are the enemies doing?"

"It looks like their ships will reach the orbit of New Shanghai soon. The Alliance fleet has not responded yet."

"Damn it, if we were on the *Robespierre*, we could reach Ganesh in an instant!" Yuri slammed her fist on a table.

Junkou had never seen his captain so restless. But he also understood.

Life reapers on a cosmic scale had entered the Desirée system. And there were billions of harvestable humans across the three planetary systems.

Kamura was muttering behind them like a madman, tapping his fingers on his knee. He was also thinking of the event that happened twenty years ago.

Then came the communication. It was Yukyung's voice.

"Captain Yuri, I think you should come here."

"Yukyung? What's going on?" said Yuri.

After that, they heard the voice of a desperate man. It was Jena.

"Yuri, Karan is acting strange! Come quickly."

Moments later, Yuri entered the cabin and saw the crew gathered around Karan. Yukyung, Desmond, Jena, and the other members of the Brotherhood. Yuri rushed to Karan's bedside.

"What happened?"

No one opened their mouth. Yuri looked at Jena, who had a blank expression, and Desmond, who looked depressed, in turn, and finally Yukyung.

Yukyung said in a trembling voice, "I was in charge this time. I tried to lay him down and give him another sedative, but his fever was boiling."

Yukyung couldn't speak any more.

Yuri turned back to Karan. "Karan?"

There was no answer.

She reached for his hand. It felt cold. "Karan Shetty?"

His complexion was pale. It was the color of a corpse.

Yuri thought she was having a nightmare. The man who had once been her lover lay unmoving. She leaned down and pressed her cheek to his face, gripping his hand tighter.

"Karan?"

He wasn't breathing.

Yuri tried to rub warmth his body. She continued to rub him and call his name.

"Karan? Karan? What are you doing? Why won't you wake up?"

With all her might, she rubbed Karan's body, like she would never stop. Desmond turned his head away involuntarily.

Unable to see this go on any longer, Jena spoke up. "Yuri, stop it. The captain is dead."

Yuri blankly shook her head. Jena grabbed her shoulder with both hands to make her stop rubbing Karan.

"The captain is dead, Yuri. You have to accept it. And you have to think about the task at hand."

Yuri turned and looked at Karan again. No tears flowed down her cheeks. In fact, she looked like she was about to burst out laughing.

Karan Shetty had left her.

Kamura came into the room. "What the hell is this…" He stopped talking when he saw Karan's body.

"Yuri," said Jena gently.

"Leave me here alone for five minutes," she said.

"Are you sure?"

"Five minutes, Jena. Can you give me five minutes?"

Jena looked at her face for a moment and then turned away. He gestured to the people who had gathered there to get out.

After they all left, only Karan and Yuri remained in the room.

She knelt next to Karan and took his hand again. She placed his hand on her forehead.

A single tear trickled down her cheek.

Danny looked back as Harry's body was loaded into the lorry. A military policeman grabbed Danny's arm and pushed him forward. He stumbled again.

Did you think this would happen just an hour ago? Danny's mind was racing as fast as his heart. *Think about it, Danny Carlos. You can't let them take you like this. Think, think, think.*

If he didn't do anything, he would die. And all the facts would disappear and the humans of the system would once again be slaughtered by aliens.

He and the military police were passing by the eastern side of the airfield. The ships waiting at the airfield took off vertically one by one. He saw the dots drifting blankly into the sky. Sura Handler had lied; the alien force was still heading for Ganesh, not New Shanghai.

A humming sound came from somewhere. A voice. Danny turned his head.

A big screen was installed in the center of the premises, and the upper body of President Soros was projected there. He was talking. Danny tried to make out what he was saying from a distance.

"Again, the Star System Defense Force will work with the aliens to defeat the rebels of Ganesh and protect your life and property. However, there may be some unrest in the process. All civilians, please stay out of the way. Please move to the areas with shelters or bunkers that are under the control of the military. You must trust the government and move. With your cooperation, the rebels will be wiped out once and for all. We've faced a difficult resistance, but the dawn of a brighter age is coming. For the citizens who always trust and support the government, the Star Defense Force will fight the rebels."

Danny noticed his A-wing parked in a corner of the airfield.

He had to run away.

But where could he go? He would be pursued. An A-wing alone couldn't escape into space. Even if he could get away from these policemen and stole the ship, they would immediately track him down. Where could he hide so they wouldn't find him?

Danny suddenly remembered he was in Altra, the capital of New Shanghai.

The Granot office building wasn't far away.

He planted his feet, refusing to move, and the policeman who was dragging him stopped. The policeman pointed his gun at Danny.

"Move, Danny Carlos."

The last sound the policeman heard was the wind.

He flew to the opposite side of the road and crashed into an alloy wall.

The air around Danny heated up. It seemed to gather toward his heart and then spread like a blade in all directions. A telekinetic storm, more powerful than ever, swept around him.

Danny thought of Joe Milligan. He remembered his eyes as he looked sadly at him in the Connecticut shopping center. He thought of the young Sean Carlos, humming as he hugged his baby boy, and he thought of Nilla. He saw Yuri Ivanova's dazzling smile in her evening dress at the party, and the bright colors that broke through her teeth, and he saw Harry Carlos's dying eyes full of remorse.

The ships tilted in the telekinetic storm. The screen broadcasting the President's face exploded, and some of the soldiers were crushed beneath it, while others scrambled to get away.

Danny breathed heavily. Exhaustion flooded his whole body. He staggered backward and looked around.

All the objects around him were broken, and soldiers fell or fainted.

Danny half-stumbled, half-ran to his A-wing. The jet's upper body opened, and Danny hurriedly climbed inside. The lid closed and the A-wing began to maneuver in auto-flight mode. He switched to manual flight mode. Grabbing the stick, he accelerated toward the sky. The A-wing tilted and swayed as it careened away from the base. Missiles and plasma flew past him.

He had only one place to go.

Dozens of ships, including the *Canberra*, *Witch Hunter*, and *Admiral Lou's* flagship, were floating over Ganesh.

Theresia tapped his fingers on the console nervously. He continued to stare at the command room screen without saying a word.

More ships began to appear. They were mostly elliptical in shape, with different features than the human ships, and they were moving at a fast speed.

They were alien ships.

And they were similar in shape to the ships that had appeared on planet Han twenty years ago.

Fumbling inside his shirt, Theresia pulled out an old gold necklace.

He called out the name of the necklace's last owner softly. "Protect me, Julia."

22.

Haneul Bravo had a gloomy expression. "How many ships?" she asked.

"About sixty ships, Commander," answered the *Moscow* pilot.

"Oh my God."

The screen was filled with black and dark gray oval-shaped ships.

Haneul's face turned white. "How long before the *Puree* arrives?"

"Based on the signal and location we encountered yesterday, another three hours or so."

The Resistance fleet was composed of a little less than fifty ships. At the vanguard were a number of cruisers and assault ships commanded by the Brotherhood. The Discarded and captured Allied ships were layered in the middle, and a number of support ships and the flagship *Moscow* were in the aft. Sky's purpose was to buy time and ensure it would be safe for Yuri and her party to return.

It was a war situation where they could not easily move, because they didn't know what the enemy's first move would be.

Moments later, the pilot reported in a tense voice, "The enemies are starting to move."

The flanks of the alien ships moved first.

"How the hell can you move like that?" murmured Haneul.

The ships glided through space at an unparalleled speed.

Theresia's communication came in. "*Moscow*, stay in the aft. We will proceed with a preemptive attack first. If there is still room, please support."

Haneul answered, "Copy that."

The Brotherhood destroyers began their advance. Theresia believed that overwhelming firepower was important to subdue an opponent of unknown power. All sorts of missiles, anti-ship guns, plasma guns, and ion cannons flew in.

"Don't give them a chance to counterattack. Just push," ordered Theresia.

The ships on both sides of the formation didn't stop warming up their guns and firing. Judy had never seen such continuous shelling.

"I'm worried that the guns of the ships will melt, Judy," said Gajin, who was on board with him.

"We'd better hope not."

The assault fighters made an open maneuver. They were tasked with entering the rear of the alien ships and conducting close-range artillery fire.

The bombardment lasted more than twenty minutes. Theresia gave the order for everyone to stop firing, and they did.

He frowned, observing the wreckage. Only a few alien ships had been destroyed; their remains floated in space. Most of the ships had taken very little damage.

"Why didn't that work?" hissed Theresia.

Little did he know, the alien ships' force captains had blocked most of the attacks.

And the counterattack began.

Beams flew from the alien ships. The same plasma, but the degree of condensation and heat were different. Some ships hit by the overwhelming level of beams exploded in an instant and split in two.

A fire soared into outer space. The wreckage of the ship floated around, along with the bodies of the crewmembers.

Some alien ships launched missiles. Theresia was astonished when he realized that the missiles had been launched by a Resistance ship. He sent a message to the entire fleet.

"Do not fire missiles and shell-type guns!"

"Why not?" asked Haneul Bravo.

"They have the ability to send physical attacks right back at us! Only use beam attacks!"

Haneul's eyes widened. "Oh my God."

She saw the missiles floating in the force field of some alien ships fly straight toward the ships of the opposing Resistance force and hit them.

"Some kind of huge kinetic field is sending the shells back toward us," said Theresia. "It's a technology we've never seen before, damn it."

In an instant, more than a dozen Resistance ships were destroyed.

The alien ships floating in the center of the formation began to move. The assault ships that had maneuvered to the rear of the alien ships stopped moving.

Theresia jumped out of his seat. "What's going on? Send communications to the assault ships."

Signals were sent, but no reply came.

"Theresia, what the hell is going on?" asked Judy over the comm link.

"I don't know. Our assault ships went out of control in an instant. They won't respond."

"Oh my God, are the aliens using an EMP field?"

"On such a huge scale? Judy, damn it. There's no hope."

Theresia's despairing voice could be heard throughout the fleet.

"This is Captain Theresia of the *Canberra*. The enemy is using a force field that stops the shells we fire and stops the approaching ships."

The enemy's fleet was quickly approaching close proximity to the *Canberra*. He had to make a decision.

"The command system is meaningless from now on. Everyone, do your best to survive."

He paused for a moment, then lifted his head. The crew had heavy faces.

"Good luck."

Theresia ended the communication.

Haneul saw the ships of the Resistance forces being crushed individually. Although only a few of the alien ships were destroyed, most of them were smashed in intact.

It seemed obvious to anyone there that the Resistance would be annihilated.

"Captain, other ships are being detected," said a fearful voice.

New ships appeared one by one on the radar. They were

the ships of mankind. Allied ships coming from New Shanghai.

"Give the order, Captain."

Haneul didn't know what order to give. "We will all be annihilated."

She looked around at the crew of the *Moscow*. She soon knew what she had to do. Conserve as much power as possible to plan for the future.

"Please spread my word to the entire fleet," she told one of her crewmembers.

Soon her trembling voice flew through the entire fleet.

"To all Discarded members and Resistance forces, listen. Abandon Ganesh and evacuate as far from the system as possible. Do it now."

That was the last command from Haneul.

After completing the internal communication, she sent the rescue signal of the *Moscow* ship to the designated coordinates. It wasn't for Joshua Kwon and Cassie Ice, nor for the Root Restorationists. There was only one person she thought of.

"Wasp, I need your help." Haneul murmured that name more earnestly than ever.

The alien ships moved toward Ganesh.

"They're coming, Ari."

The bombardment of alien ships toward Ganesh began. The Resistance forces on the ground and the army of the former governor of the Allied forces did their best to activate the air defense system. However, the shelling from the alien ships was merciless. Several towns in Ganesh were hit hard. Soon some of the alien ships began to descend.

Residents of Ganesh City started screaming and

running. The city center was plunged into chaos. Traffic was paralyzed, and vehicles and A-wings were left abandoned.

Jinsoo trembled as he stared at the scene from afar. He felt as if he had returned to the past. "I never thought I'd see a sight like this again."

Ari knew he was back on the planet Han twenty years ago. His trauma and old feelings were rising to the surface.

The emotions felt by living beings when they came face to face with death.

Ari grabbed his shoulder. She appealed in an earnest voice. "Please, you don't have time to be like this. We have to move. No one can save them but us!"

Jinsoo rolled his eyes to look at her. He seemed as if he was staring at something she couldn't see. Memories of the past. Ari wanted to hug him, but she also wanted to hit him.

"Wake up!" she shouted.

Jinsoo's eyes slowly focused. He nodded.

"You're right, Ari." He laughed softly. "It's not our style to sit still and wait for death."

They didn't want to think about what awaited them.

A call came into the Granot office, and Yeoreum's secretary answered it. Not many people remained in the building.

"Ma'am," said her secretary when she answered the call. "There is a visitor who would like to meet with you."

Yeoreum huffed in annoyance. "Wang Fei, isn't it late for someone to come calling?"

"I'm sorry, boss. But he says it's urgent—"

Yeoreum sighed. "Who is the visitor?"

"Captain Danny Carlos of the Allied forces."

"What? Why is he here at this hour?"

"I don't know, boss. He says he needs to see you right away."

Yeoreum considered it for a while. "Fine. Bring him up."

"Yes, ma'am."

While Wang Fei was gone, Yeoreum pulled out a mirror from her desk drawer, checked her makeup, and adjusted her outfit. After a while, an AI voice told her that someone was outside her door.

"A visitor has arrived."

"Let him in."

The door opened and Danny Carlos entered.

He looked like he'd just woken up. His hair was messy and his uniform was caked in dirt. Yeoreum was a little startled, but on the outside, she spoke without showing any disorientation.

"Hello, Carlos." She got up from her seat "You look very tired."

"It happens."

Yeoreum nodded. "What made you want to see me? At this time, too? Do you know that martial law has been imposed on the entire planet?"

"I know."

His complexion was rather pale. Danny's eyes twinkled like a madman.

"I won't say much, boss. I need your help."

"What kind of help?" she asked.

"Lend me a ship with a warp drive."

Yeoreum observed Danny for a moment. She sensed something. "Are you being chased, Captain?"

Danny didn't say anything. Yeoreum figured that meant she was right.

"Okay. So, you need my help?"

"That's right."

"Why do you think I'll help you?"

Danny sighed. He pulled out his gun and aimed at Yeoreum.

"Because if you don't, I'll kill you."

Yeoreum's mouth pinched at the sides.

Danny said earnestly, "Please, please help me."

They took the elevator down to the 25th basement floor, which Danny had visited the last time he came to the office. Standing behind Yeoreum, Danny pointed the gun hidden in the pocket of his coat at her back.

As they approached the underground hangar, an Android G approached.

"Hello, boss. What's going on at this hour?"

"Open the door, G. I want to check out the goods for a moment," said Yeoreum tightly.

"At this hour? Is there a problem?"

"No problem, G. I just feel like seeing them."

"Would you like me to send you a report analyzing the status of products to the office? That way, you will be able to scan them more quickly."

"G, I don't need that. Please open the door."

The short-haired android bobbed his head. For some reason, Danny thought it looked creepy.

"Okay, boss." The android's iris glowed orange. "I have turned off security. You can enter."

"Thanks, G."

Yeoreum and Danny headed into the hangar. Danny glanced back at G, who looked at him with an expressionless face. Danny turned his head.

The hangar was filled with over a dozen prototype ships.

The ships were well maintained and radiating a clean color.

"There aren't any Kudo class ships right now," said Yeoreum. "You took one, and the Allied forces have already taken over the rest of the mass production."

"Then the Soros class will have to do. Can I drive the ship by myself?"

"Soros's autopilot can do most of the calculations and tasks by itself. It's been tested and can handle any flight."

"Glad to hear it. Enter the embarkation protocol and hand it over to me, boss."

Yeoreum bit her lip and put her right hand on the handy tool to manipulate it. After a few moments, Danny confirmed that the new protocol and authority had been transferred to his handy tool. It was the control authority of the Soros ship. He ordered the ship to be powered on. Soon, the light of a medium-sized ship in the left corner of the hangar lit up, and the hum of its engine reverberated through the room.

Yeoreum said in a cold voice, "I never knew a Connecticut hero could be so mean, Captain."

"I'm sorry, boss, but I have to get out of here."

Yeoreum didn't say anything. Danny opened his mouth, then shook his head and started toward the ship.

"Stop, Danny Carlos!"

A group of privately armed guards poured into the hangar.

Danny wrapped one arm around Yeoreum's neck, pulled out a gun, and thrust it into her temple. *What a cheap villain I am*, he thought.

"If you value the life of Granot's president, then you'd better not to do anything foolish," he said to the heavily armed guards who surrounded him.

A man stepped out in front of the armed guards. Danny recognized him as Dr. Cheng.

"Get your hands off the boss, Captain."

Danny was startled by the bitter rage in his voice.

"The news that you killed Commander Harry Carlos and fled has spread across the entire continent. You are the most wanted person on New Shanghai."

Yeoreum was struggling to breathe in Danny's grasp.

Dr. Cheng spoke in a clear tone. "I reported your location to the Allies. Your actions will only increase your guilt. Put down your gun."

Danny raised the gun to the ceiling and fired. *Bang!*

Dr. Cheng's face hardened even more.

"If you block my way, the boss will die," spat Danny. He hated that he was treating them this way, but he didn't have any choice. "Let me through."

Dr. Cheng stared at him quietly. Danny aimed his gun at him, then brought the gun to Yeoreum's head.

"Hurry."

Dr. Cheng muttered, "You motherfucker." To the guards, he said, "Let him go."

The guards stepped aside. Danny kept looking at them as he carefully stepped sideways toward the Soros ship with Yeoreum. Dr. Cheng and the guards stared at him, and Danny kept moving closer to Soros as he kept them in check.

"Captain Carlos, release the boss!"

"Not yet!" Danny shouted.

He approached the ship with Yeoreum, continuing to glance at the guards. Yeoreum tried to resist him, but his power was too strong.

Danny and Yeoreum neared the Soros ship. The

entrance door slid down.

"Danny Carlos!" called Dr. Cheng, starting to run to him.

Danny threw Yeoreum into the ship's elevator. He then fired a gun at Dr. Cheng's lower torso.

"Father!" Yeoreum cried.

Dr. Cheng faltered and fell. He groaned.

"You bastard!" Yeoreum threw a slap at Danny.

As soon as he got on the platform, the elevator went up at a frightening speed, taking them straight to the Soros class command room. Yeoreum glared at Danny.

"Dr. Cheng was your father?" he said with a little embarrassment. "I didn't know."

"You motherfucker! I'll kill you!"

The intelligent and calm face of the beautiful woman was nowhere to be found; in its place was a look of venom. Danny clicked his tongue. Of course, he had no excuses.

"I'm sorry, boss. But it won't affect the life of the doctor. I purposely shot him in an area that wouldn't do much damage."

Yeoreum rushed at him. Danny could feel her telekinetic powers coming to life. He sighed, then struck Yeoreum hard in the back of the head.

She let out a gasp and fell into Danny's arms. He put her in the passenger seat and fastened her belt.

"I'm sorry, but I'm taking you hostage. And you won't be able to kill me easily."

She didn't answer.

Danny set to work turning on autopilot.

Soros broke through the hangar roof and soared toward the ground level. It took off while destroying the structure of several floors.

Danny changed direction as soon as *Soros* reached the ground. *Soros* broke the glass at the entrance of the Granot office building and flew toward the sky.

Several ships appeared on the radar. They were chasing him.

After counting to three, Danny pressed the button for the warp drive and pulled the lever.

A short, silver-haired man in the uniform of an Allied general looked down on the burning planet's surface from above Ganesh. The man stood on the bridge of a warp-drive ship named after him. He gave control of the ship to his lieutenant and headed to the captain's office.

Arriving at the office, he took off his uniform and put on a tunic. The man took a bottle of wine from the refrigerator, poured it into a glass, and sat down in a rocking chair. When he pressed a few buttons on the console attached to his desk, the screen showed him planet Ganesh and alien ships pouring down from outer space.

The man raised his glass in a toast and drank the wine in one gulp. The refreshing, slightly sour taste lifted his spirits.

Amon Soros set the glass on the desk, then clasped his fingers together. A smile played on his lips, but his eyes were so serious that they looked a little sad.

"It's a wonderful sight, isn't it, Kiliman?" he said.

He was talking to himself, but Amon didn't care. He continued speaking as if the other person had already answered.

"Isn't it? Don't you look young? It's been twenty years."

He burst into laughter.

"Not everyone thinks so…but sometimes I really miss

you. You were the only man who could understand me."

Amon covered his face with both hands. His breathing became heavy; his back went up and down. Soon he lowered his hands again and drank another glass of wine.

"How about it? I thought I'd miss you, so I played it again."

The whole planet became a sea of fire. It started in the northern hemisphere, and then emerged in the southern hemisphere at the opposite point. The twinkling flames were reminiscent of multicolored lotus lanterns flying in the night sky on festival days.

"I miss you, Kiliman. I miss you so much." Deep regret filled the President's voice. "I'll make a toast to the days of no return. Let's have a drink."

He poured the glass and lifted it high. He hummed and offered a toast.

"A drink for Kiliman Ivanov!"

He emptied his glass and poured another.

"And a drink for your brave daughter!"

The President filled the glass once again.

"Let's have another drink for the returning Worshippers of the Left Hand!"

The President tilted the glass toward the burning Ganesh. Fire engulfed the entire planet, and aliens were slaughtering humans.

His laughter grew louder. He looked at the burning planet. He put down his glass and cleared his throat a few times.

He opened his mouth. A voice came out. At first, he paused, but soon the scales of the singing came back into place as if they were playing data. He was satisfied. The sound of singing filled the captain's room.

… The child who could not sleep asked, "Mom, what's that light?"

The child was pitiful, and the mother lied.

"Baby, those are the angels that came down. They are the angels of light who have come down to take the good sleepless children to dreamland. Look. Can't you see the twinkling light from the wings of the angels wandering over there?"

"Mom, angels breathe fire from their mouths."

"Looks like angels are taking the bad guys away. Angels punish those who do bad things and reward good people like us."

"But Mother, the angels saw us. They're coming for us."

"Baby, go to sleep now. When you wake up, we'll all be in heaven together. You and I will run and play in heaven's green and flowery garden."

"Mom, the angels saw us. Angels breathe fire. I think we did something bad."

"Dear baby, angels only catch bad people. So, do you want to go to sleep? When we wake up, we will be in heaven. Go to sleep now. Forget all the pain in the world, my dear sweetheart. Please sleep in the eternal darkness, before this fire eats us up. Before it burns up our souls, go to dreamland, my dear."

Epilogue

The ship flew through the darkness full of dust and microscopic particles, passing through several celestial bodies. The first thing the ship met after passing the nameless dwarf planets was a rocky planet. It was a fairly large, faintly lit planet with a frozen crust, quietly floating in space.

As the man looked at the rocky planet so isolated from its star, he thought, *Just like me*. The frozen planet's mass was considerable. The man realized that it acted as a visitor's gateway to the outermost parts of the system.

The ship was continued sailing at sub-lightspeed toward the center of the planetary system, where they were meant to be. Their current location was the result of a minor calculation error when setting the route. Of course, if there had been a really noticeable error, they would've ended up in another system entirely.

When the man said that aloud, his friend replied, "Isn't this better? We get to take a cruise through the solar system. This is the world we lost."

The man nodded, thinking that his friend made sense.

The ship passed the outermost planets at 500 hours of voyage. After 900 hours, gas planets came into view. They were planets with blue oceans of methane. *If you go down there, you won't be too bored*, he thought with a chuckle. Of course, they would freeze during the descent.

At 1094 hours, they passed the giant gas planets with rings. One of the rocky moons of the outer gas planet also had an ocean of methane. They saw structures installed in the crust there—abandoned bases from an old civilization.

They were nearing their destination.

The man looked at the Great Red Spot on the second giant gas planet, which filled the bridge screen. The planet moved in real time, emitting blue and red light like marble, like the work of a surrealist painter. He estimated how long this world would have lasted on his own principles.

"Do you think these celestial bodies know what happened 600 years ago?" he asked his friend.

"I don't know. What do you think?"

"No. It must have been an instant moment."

"Hmm, you seem to be getting more and more sentimental."

The man did not respond to his friend's words. He stared intently at the Red Spot.

At 1142 hours, the ship encountered an asteroid belt. They slowed down and passed by, crushing the asteroids. Not much left now.

They came to a planet covered in red sand. The man looked at it for a moment and then turned his head. Not much farther. He was now completely awake.

After 1170 hours, the planet finally appeared.

The man looked at the blue ball reflected through the

screen. The voyage was almost over. Numerous passengers all came out of the bridge and stared at the screen. In the distance, shining planets were sparsely visible. This was because of the vacuum on the outside of Orion's arm viewed from this direction. Now, the planetary system they belonged to was not the center of the galaxy, so they were not used to seeing this part of space.

We made it, the man thought, his heart beating fast.

His friend came up to him and said the same thing. "We've arrived."

"What should we do now?"

The friend shrugged. "How about we enjoy the view a little more? That planet won't run away."

Looking at his friend's face, the man nodded. His friend put his hand on his shoulder and said, "I'm thinking of getting some cocoa. Would you like some too?"

"Yes, thank you."

The friend nodded and walked away. The man followed his back with his eyes and then looked at the screen again.

His friend had looked at the planet and acted as if it wasn't anything extraordinary, but the man knew how thrilled he must have been. He'd been dreaming of coming here for decades.

The man stopped trying to capture all the shapes of the continents of the planet currently floating in front of them. Indeed, this planet wouldn't run away.

But the man had run away. From her. From her and her daughter.

The man murmured, "Cassie, can you believe it? I'm on Earth."

He had no idea what they would find on this world in front of him, the world his ancestors had left long ago.

But whatever it was, he had a feeling they were in for an adventure.

End of Book Two

Author's Note

I think it's more difficult to write the author's story than writing a novel itself. And I am embarrassed to try to tell my story to you now. First of all, the first story I prepared has come to an end.

Maybe you think there is a cliffhanger at the end of the book. I didn't think of it as a cliffhanger when I wrote the book. I think that it has a sense of completeness in itself, and the completeness is compressed and revealed in the final scene through the repeated themes and truths of the book. From the first chapter to the last, the writing explores why a tragic event occurred twenty years ago and what was behind it. Even at the climax, the tragedy of the past continues, and the worshipper of the left hand reappears. The ending itself may seem like a cliffhanger at first glance, but in that sense, I think it presents a single conclusion, the triumph of evil that has been waiting for decades.

Good and evil, the two constantly compete and fight. Neither good nor evil is eternal. As an author I just describe and write it.

I would like to meet you with the next book soon. Thank you to the readers who have bought my books for a little fun in these uncertain days.

About the Author

Min Hyesung majored in English Literature and Political Science. He is interested in the manifestation of the human nature and the inhuman reality in situations and in human eras, and the story of the human being in those situations and eras, and would like to realize this in literature. He is planning various works across several genres, such as sci-fi, fantasy literature, and hard-boiled.

www.ingramcontent.com/pod-product-compliance
Lightning Source LLC
Chambersburg PA
CBHW060929190726
48286CB00002B/694